Daniel smiled and took a beer out of the fridge.

His brother Quinn, then his father, had come by to talk about Antonia. All that was missing was a call from Cater or Cory. Or Beth.

That would come, he assured himself—as soon as one of them talked to Quinn. But Daniel knew he didn't really mind. His family's concern was warming. Besides, he rather liked everyone knowing he was seeing Antonia Campbell.

He smiled again, taking a swig of beer. *Talk about feeling like a teenager again.* He realized that he was grinning at the wall like an idiot, but the fact only made him grin harder. He hadn't felt this good in years. *And he intended to make damn sure he continued feeling that way.*

Dear Reader,

The excitement continues in Intimate Moments. First of all, this month brings the emotional and exciting conclusion of A YEAR OF LOVING DANGEROUSLY. In *Familiar Stranger,* Sharon Sala presents the final confrontation with the archvillain known as Simon—and you'll finally find out who he really is. You'll also be there as Jonah revisits the woman he's never forgotten and decides it's finally time to make some important changes in his life.

Also this month, welcome back Candace Camp to the Intimate Moments lineup. Formerly known as Kristin James, this multitalented author offers a *Hard-Headed Texan* who lives in A LITTLE TOWN IN TEXAS, which will enthrall readers everywhere. Paula Detmer Riggs returns with *Daddy with a Badge,* another installment in her popular MATERNITY ROW miniseries—and next month she's back with *Born a Hero,* the lead book in our new Intimate Moments continuity, FIRSTBORN SONS. Complete the month with *Moonglow, Texas,* by Mary McBride, Linda Castillo's *Cops and...Lovers?* and new author Susan Vaughan's debut book, *Dangerous Attraction.*

By the way, don't forget to check out our Silhouette Makes You a Star contest on the back of every book.

We hope to see you next month, too, when not only will FIRSTBORN SONS be making its bow, but we'll also be bringing you a brand-new TALL, DARK AND DANGEROUS title from award-winning Suzanne Brockmann. For now...enjoy!

Leslie J. Wainger
Executive Senior Editor

Please address questions and book requests to:
Silhouette Reader Service
U.S.: 3010 Walden Ave., P.O. Box 1325, Buffalo, NY 14269
Canadian: P.O. Box 609, Fort Erie, Ont. L2A 5X3

CANDACE CAMP

Hard-Headed Texan

Silhouette®

INTIMATE MOMENTS™

Published by Silhouette Books

America's Publisher of Contemporary Romance

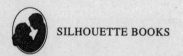

SILHOUETTE BOOKS

ISBN 0-373-27151-4

HARD-HEADED TEXAN

This edition published by arrangement with Harlequin Books S.A.

Visit Silhouette at www.eHarlequin.com

Printed in U.S.A.

Books by Candace Camp

Silhouette Intimate Moments

**Hard-Headed Texan* #1081

Silhouette Books

Maternity Leave
*"Tabloid Baby"

*A Little Town in Texas

Previously written under the name Kristin James

Silhouette Intimate Moments

Dreams of Evening #1
The Amber Sky #17
Morning Star #45
Secret Fires #69
Worlds Apart #89
Cutter's Lady #125
A Very Special Favor #136
Salt of the Earth #385
The Letter of the Law #393

Silhouette Desire

Once in a Blue Moon #962
The Last Groom on Earth #986

CANDACE CAMP,

a *USA Today* bestselling author and former attorney, is married to a Texan, and they have a daughter who has been bitten by the acting bug. Candace's family and her writing keep her busy, but when she does have free time, she loves to read. In addition to her contemporary romances, she has written a number of historicals, which are currently being published by MIRA Books.

Chapter 1

The phone rang, startling Antonia awake. She sat bolt upright, heart pounding. Beside her the cat stood up, looking at her balefully for disturbing her nap, then stalked off. Antonia blinked, her sleep-fogged mind adjusting to her surroundings. It was the clinic, she told herself. There was an emergency at the clinic. The telephone shrilled again, and she picked up the receiver.

"Dr. Campbell," she answered, relieved that she had managed to make her voice come out calm and cool. She didn't want anyone here to know that the least thing could make her panic.

There was no sound on the other end of the line, and she repeated her words, more loudly. Still there was no answer, even though the phone had the sound of a live connection.

"Hello?" she said, fighting down the upsurge of

panic-nerves in her chest. ''Who is this? Can I help you?''

Still there was no reply, and Antonia slammed down the receiver. Her hands were shaking, and there was a tight, cold knot in the center of her chest.

It wasn't him, she reminded herself. It was probably just a wrong number or one of those strange connections that went awry—it happened with some regularity when the caller was using a cell phone. The silence on the end of the line did not mean that it was Alan. Alan did not know where she was; there was no reason to think that he did. This was just blind, unreasoning, atavistic fear, and she refused to give in to it.

Antonia took a deep, calming breath and went over all the reasons why she was safe now. Alan was in Virginia, and she was here; he did not know where she lived. It had been years since their divorce. He had not bothered her since she moved to Texas.

Still, she got out of bed and went to the front door, checking to make sure that it was locked and the chain was on. The little red light of the security monitor was blinking, showing that the security system was in effect. She went to the front room window of her small house and lifted the edge of the drapes to peer outside. It was dark outside, though beginning to lighten into a predawn grayness. She could make out the shapes of the trees in the front yard and her SUV parked in the narrow, old-fashioned driveway beside her house.

She would have preferred a house with an attached garage, but the charm of the 1920s-style bungalow had outweighed other considerations, and the passage of years had lessened her bunker mentality. A security system, an old neighborhood imbued with small-town friendliness and nosiness, her own hard-won vigilance—these were enough, she'd decided. She could not let her entire life be ruled by the fear that Alan might find her; if she did, she was letting him control her still.

Antonia walked around the small house, checking each of the windows and the back door to make sure that they were all locked. Reassured, she turned on the coffeemaker, already prepared the night before for ease in getting ready in the morning, and sat down at the kitchen table to wait.

It was pointless trying to go back to bed, she knew. Even though she had calmed down and was reassured that she was safe, it would take her a long time to go back to sleep, and her alarm was set to go off in thirty minutes. A veterinarian in a small ranching community kept early hours, just like the owners of the animals to which she tended. Antonia was usually in the office by seven and often on the road to one ranch or another soon after that.

That morning she arrived even earlier, before the receptionist or either of the technicians. Dr. Carmichael, the other veterinarian, never came in before ten o'clock. It was the reason he had brought in another vet, he had told her—the heavy workload and the early mornings were getting to be too much for him, and at seventy-two years old, he had decided to take life a little easier. Only the night watchman, Miguel, was there. A shy young man who loved to read, he was a perfect person to be on night duty with the animals. He was intelligent; only the fact that he came from a large, poor family had kept him from attending college. He knew as much as most of the techs, and he also had a rapport with the animals that was invaluable. A self-proclaimed insomniac, he had no trouble staying awake all night, and the long hours alone and doing nothing except making hourly rounds did not bore him as they would have most people. He was quite happy to read one of his books.

"Good morning, Dr. Campbell," he said, coming out of the kennel door when she drove up.

"Hi, Miguel. How's it going?" Antonia stepped out of her SUV, not bothering to lock it, another habit she had gotten into since moving to Angel Eye three months ago. Because their offices contained drugs, as well as for the safety of the animals, the clinic had a state-of-the-art security system, but there had never been a break-in—or even an attempted one. Everyone who parked in the clinic lot was more interested in finding a shady spot to protect their vehicle from the broiling Texas sun than in locking their doors.

"It's okay." Miguel knew that her question was more than rhetorical. "All the animals got through the night, even Dingo." Dingo was a mixed-breed dog with liver problems, and it had been touch-and-go with him all day yesterday. Owned and much loved by a family with two little girls, Dingo had captured most of the clinic staff's hearts, as well.

"Good. Well, let me get into my lab coat, and we'll make the rounds."

"Sure, Dr. Campbell." Miguel grinned shyly, not quite meeting Antonia's eyes.

Antonia was aware that she intimidated the young

man. He was shy to begin with, but the fact that she was a towering six feet tall, with the cool, blond good looks of an East Coast society princess, had turned the poor kid nearly speechless when she first came to the clinic. Antonia often had that effect on people, so she was not surprised. She didn't try to be distant or icy; in fact, her basic nature was warm. But she was by nature and experience somewhat reserved, and the years of training in the proper demeanor expected of a young lady that she had received from her mother—"a lady does not cry in public," "a lady doesn't show a vulgar display of excitement," "a lady does not display unseemly curiosity"—had given her a vaguely aloof air that she did not know how to shake. Even in the casual shirt and jeans that she typically wore on and off the job, she still looked like someone who should be on her way to a Junior League meeting. Today, for instance, she wore jeans and a plain blue shirt, with her hair pulled back and arranged in a practical French braid and only the barest hint of makeup on her face, yet she was somehow elegant.

Antonia usually dealt with her looks by ignoring them. Once she was ready to go in the morning, she rarely glanced in a mirror the rest of the day. Her clothes were invariably practical. Her skin care regimen consisted of little beyond simple cleaning, moisturizing and frequent applications of sunscreen to keep her fair skin from burning. Her technician and friend Rita Delgado, whose devotion to skin care and makeup was profound, was frequently appalled by Antonia's blasé attitude.

"What is sickening," she would say, shaking her

head, "is that you do almost nothing and still look the way you do!"

Antonia went to her office and pulled on a clean lab coat from the closet, then walked down the hall to the locked door that led to the back part of the clinic, where the sick animals were kept. Miguel was waiting for her there, and they started on their rounds, beginning with Dingo, who was miraculously hanging on.

She had checked over only three animals, approving one for dismissal that day, when the door from the main office burst open and Lilian, the receptionist, bustled in. Lilian, a middle-aged widow of very precise habits, was often the first person to reach the clinic. She liked to have the coffee made and her book work done before the clinic opened at seven-thirty. Lilian had a rather militaristic bent, Antonia thought, and she wanted to have her supplies lined up and her plans in order before she did battle with their clients.

"Dr. Campbell!" Lilian's soft-featured face, so at odds with her crisp, no-nonsense personality, was creased with concern. "Daniel Sutton just called. He's having trouble with one of his mares. He said to come right away. She's been in labor for a while, and she's losing ground."

"Daniel Sutton?" Antonia asked, already unbuttoning her lab coat and starting back toward the front of the clinic. "The ranch I went to last week?"

"No, that's Marshall. His father. Daniel's on the same road, though, about ten minutes further west. Marshall Sutton's a cattleman, but Daniel raises horses. He's knowledgeable. If he says there's something wrong, then there is."

"Okay. I'll take the mobile." Antonia hung her lab coat on a hook beside the back door, listening as Lilian gave her detailed directions to Daniel Sutton's horse farm. She took the key to the clinic's mobile vet truck from another hook. It was the task of whoever drove the truck last to make sure that it was filled with gas and stocked with supplies so that it was always ready to go the next day.

She ran lightly down the steps and crunched across the gravel lot to where the mobile truck sat parked beneath a shade tree. Dr. Carmichael had told her many tales of his early days in the area, when he had driven around to the nearby ranches in his old International Harvester truck, a forerunner of the modern SUVs, with a stock of supplies in the back that he would need for his large animal practice. Today, of course, like most vets who practiced in rural areas, he had a modern mobile, a truck equipped with a shell, looking much like one of the smaller motor homes, in which there were sinks, refrigeration for some of the medicines and samples, and nearly every kind of instrument or medicine needed for working on animals in the field. It was generally far more practical for the vet to go to the horse or cow than for the animal to be loaded into a trailer and brought to the veterinarian.

Time, of course, was of the essence when a mare was having problems foaling, and the long distances between farms and ranches here ate up that precious time, so Antonia stepped on the gas when she left the outskirts of Angel Eye, bringing the truck up to eighty. She doubted that any sheriff's deputy in this ranching community would interfere with a speeding vet on her way to save a horse.

Lilian's directions were as precise as she was, and Antonia had no trouble finding the Sutton horse farm. She turned off the highway onto a graveled road, blocked by a mechanized steel gate. She pushed the button on the small raised platform, and almost immediately the gate began to swing open.

"I'm in the foaling pens, Doc," a deep male voice, tight with worry, said over the intercom. "Better step on it. She's in a bad way."

Antonia stepped on the accelerator and started up the long drive. Automatically she noted the details of the farm as she drove toward the house and barn in the distance. It was obviously a working farm—there were none of the expensive decorative touches that marked the rich hobbyist horse farms. Everything was plain and serviceable, from the front gate to the black metal fences to the old farmhouse at the end of the drive. However, there was nothing shabby or ill-kempt about it, either. The fences, the road, the barn, the paddocks, even the two horse trailers sitting beside the barn—all were in good repair and of good quality. It was a neatly kept place, and the horses in the pasture beside the road looked equally well taken care of.

She pulled to a stop between the barn and the lower-roofed stables and hopped out of the truck. Grabbing her doctor's bag, she hurried toward the stables, presuming that the foaling pens were there. As she did so, a tall man came out of the building, squinting in the sun. He raised a hand to shield his eyes, stared for a moment without moving, then came toward her at a lope.

He was long-legged, with a lean, muscled build that came from years of hard work rather than an intimate acquaintance with weight-training machines. Tall and broad-shouldered, he wore boots, worn blue jeans and a white short-sleeved T-shirt, and he looked so unutterably male that Antonia's breath caught in her throat. She stopped where she was, a little taken aback by her own reaction. Tight jeans and a wide chest didn't usually make her stomach flutter anymore, and she had seen plenty of cowboys since moving to Texas. None of them, however, had sent this jolt of pure, instinctive lust shooting straight down through her.

"Who the hell are you?" he demanded, his dark brows drawn together in a deep frown, as he stopped a few feet from her. "Where's Doc?"

He glanced toward the veterinary truck, then back at her. He was a big man, taller by several inches than Antonia, who was accustomed to looming over most men. He wore no hat, and his hair was thick and black and a trifle shaggy. His skin was tanned from years of exposure to the sun, and there were deep sun lines at the corners of his dark eyes. He was handsome and just as intensely masculine up close as he had appeared at a distance.

Much to Antonia's astonished dismay, she simply looked at him, unable to speak.

"Damn it!" the man went on. "I told her I needed Dr. Carmichael. Didn't she understand? The foal's in the wrong position. I gotta have a vet, not some tech fresh out of school!"

Antonia stiffened at his words, a quick rush of anger coming to her rescue. "I *am* the vet," she told him crisply and extended her hand, pleased to see that it didn't shake despite the bizarre inner turmoil that afflicted her.

The man stared at her, his jaw dropping comically. "What?"

"I'm the vet. Dr. Carmichael's new associate. I am Dr. Campbell." She dropped her hand, unsure whether shock or simple rudeness had kept him from shaking her hand. "Now, where's your mare?"

"But you can't be—" he said, a stunned look on his face. "You're a girl."

"I will take that as a compliment to my youthful appearance rather than a male chauvinist remark," Antonia said coolly. "However, I *am* the vet. Dr. Carmichael needed someone younger to help with his practice. I take the early morning calls."

The man let out a brief, vivid curse. "We're talking about a horse here, not a cat or dog. You can't—"

"In fact, horses are my specialty, so you're in luck," Antonia went on, struggling to keep a hold on her temper.

"Damn it, I'm not losing my best mare because Carmichael decided to go all politically correct and hire a woman vet!"

"You won't lose that horse because of me!" Antonia shot back, fury shooting up in her. "I am fully qualified to—"

"A woman doesn't have the strength to doctor a horse. I've seen big men who couldn't—"

"In case you haven't noticed," Antonia bit out, "I

am scarcely delicate. I am six feet tall and I work out. I can handle a horse. Usually I use my brains to overcome the difference in strength, and if brains won't do it, I could turn it over to you. How's that?''

A light flared in his eyes, and he came a long step closer, looming over her. Antonia was not about to be intimidated, and she, too, stepped forward, so that they were now so close she could see the thick dark lashes that ringed his eyes, making their dark brown color appear almost black.

She looked him straight in the eyes, putting her hands on her hips pugnaciously, and said, ''Dr. Carmichael is not here. I am. Now, I can leave and you can wait until Dr. Carmichael comes into the clinic and can drive out here, by which time your stubbornness will probably have cost you a mare and a foal. Or you can show me your mare and let me try to save them. Which do you want to do?''

A vein pulsed at his temple, and for a moment Antonia thought that Sutton was going to explode, but then he stepped back. ''This way,'' he said shortly, and turned and walked back into the stables. Antonia followed him.

The mare was obviously in trouble. A splendid bay quarterhorse, with a white stripe down the center of her face, she stood with head lowered and feet spread apart. She was shivering, and her body was covered with sweat. Antonia took in the details of the stall automatically as she examined the mother, even as she had noticed the condition of the farm. Here, too, all was in order and prepared. The foaling stall was clean and floored with fresh straw, and several buckets stood at the ready, along with a supply of towels, and a shelf containing various bottles and tubes and a box of latex gloves. A large sink stood a few feet away, between this and another foaling stall, and at it were a nail brush and antiseptic soap. No matter how obnoxious the owner might be, he ran a good farm.

Talking soothingly to the mare, Antonia ran a calming hand down her neck and side, moving around to the back to examine her. ''When did she go into labor?''

''During the night,'' Sutton said, wiping the back of his arm across his forehead. Antonia saw, now that the anger had subsided from it, that weariness and worry stamped his face. ''Five o'clock, maybe,'' he told her in a deep, rumbling voice. ''She started waxing up yesterday evening, and I knew it would be coming soon. I slept on a cot in the other stall. I checked her right after her water bag broke, and I couldn't find the foal's head, so I knew it was turned around. I called the clinic, and I've been walking her around.'' He paused, then went on. ''She's my best mare, and the sire is Garson's Evening Star at Mason Farms. It should be a good foal.'' He sighed and looked at Antonia. ''I don't want to lose that mare.''

''I'll do my best to save both of them,'' Antonia said, softening a little at the undercurrent of emotion in his voice. This man wasn't just talking about investments; he obviously loved his animals, and as far as Antonia was concerned, that fact made up for a multitude of sins. ''Okay, let's get to work.''

She went to the sink and began to scrub her hands.

It was obvious that Sutton was right. The foal was turned around. It was trying to emerge; one tiny hoof protruded from the mare. But it was a rear hoof, instead of the two front hooves that should come out first in a normal delivery. The poor mare, in obvious pain, was struggling to deliver. The first thing Antonia did was examine the mare, reaching in to locate the foal's head and forelegs. That in itself was difficult enough to do, but she finally determined that its head was twisted to the side, and the foal was more or less wedged sideways.

"You're right. I'll have to turn it," she said, explaining the position of the foal as she once again scrubbed her hands and arm. "First I'm going to give her a tranquilizer to calm her down, as well as an epidural. This will take a while."

Once she had administered the drugs, she went to work to turn the foal inside its mother. It was a long, tedious process, for she had to find the head and pull it back, as well as push and pull and twist until the foal was in the correct position, forelegs and head facing forward. Time after time, she tugged on the muzzle to no avail. She could not find one of the forelegs, and when she did, it slipped from her grasp.

Finally, however, she managed to get the leg secured with an obstetrical chain around it, then grasped the muzzle and wiggled and pulled until it slid around to the correct position. "I've got it!"

She began to pull, and slowly the foal slid forward until its forelegs and the tip of its muzzle emerged. Behind her Sutton let out a whoop. Antonia dropped her arm; it felt like a lead weight, numb from the strain. She shook it a little to get the feeling back, then began to pull again. The foal stuck at the chest and shoulders. It was large, and the mare was weak and tired, barely able to stand. Antonia was afraid that the mare would go down at any moment, and she was certainly no longer capable of expelling the foal.

Sutton moved up beside Antonia and grasped the muzzle and one foreleg. Antonia glanced up at him. He winked, surprising her, and said, ''Looks like this is *my* specialty, as you pointed out earlier.''

Antonia had to grin, and she reached up to take the other foreleg. They began to pull again. It was a stubborn animal, big and slippery, and the two of them had to pull mightily, but then suddenly the shoulders popped through, and a moment later the foal was out, still wrapped in its amniotic membrane.

''Yes!'' Antonia cried, triumph surging through her as Sutton gently laid the little animal down on the ground, close to its mother's head.

She squatted down beside the man to strip the membrane from around the foal's face and mouth. The mare would do the rest. Sutton turned to Antonia, a huge smile breaking across his face, and she grinned back at him.

''We did it!'' he exclaimed, and as they stood up, he suddenly reached out and swung her up into his arms, whirling her around in a paroxysm of joy. They were both filthy, their shirts and arms covered with blood and amniotic fluid, but neither of them cared. The joy of bringing life into the world filled them. Antonia laughed, exhilarated, curling her arms around his shoulders as he spun her.

In the next moment she became aware of the reality of his body against hers. His hard chest pressed into her breasts; his arms were around her like a lover's. She could feel the dampness of his sweat against her skin. A sudden, fierce desire slammed through her, almost frightening in its intensity. Antonia wanted to kiss him, to press herself against his muscular body. She wanted to taste the salt of his skin, to rub her face against his hair, to breathe in the healthy masculine smell of him.

Her breath caught in her throat. *What in the world was she doing!* She stiffened, embarrassment sweeping through her. *This was a client!* And her behavior was anything but professional.

Sutton seemed to become aware of the peculiarity of their situation in the same moment. Quickly he set her down and stepped back.

"I...ah..." He fixed his eyes on a point just over her shoulder. "Sorry. Got a little carried away, I guess."

"Yes. This kind of thing doesn't happen every day," Antonia agreed, trying to smooth over the awkward moment. Her heart pounding against her ribs, she turned back to the mare, who was now engaged in licking her foal clean. The foal lay there, adjusting to its new world, its mother's lifeblood still filling it through the umbilical cord. Antonia never cut the cord right away, as it would deprive the foal of much-needed nourishment.

"It looks as if everything's proceeding normally," she went on, aware that her voice sounded a trifle prissy, but she felt as though she had to say something, with the sudden, awkward silence settling around them.

"Yeah. I—usually Doc uses the shower out here in the barn to clean up. But—" He glanced doubtfully down the wide hallway. "Maybe you ought to use the one in the house. I'll take this one. I mean...that is, if you have something to change into. I could loan you a shirt, of course, but..." His eyes fell to her slender legs, encased in denim. "'Course you're pretty tall. I reckon you could, you know, wear something of mine...if you wanted...you could roll them up— Oh, Lord, why don't you just shoot me and shut me up before I make a complete fool of myself?"

Antonia had to smile. "A shower would be very nice, thank you. I appreciate it. I'm sure the one here in the barn is perfectly fine. And I carry a change of clothes in the truck. Unfortunately for the state of my clothes, I often wind up looking like this."

They waited for the expulsion of the afterbirth, to make sure the mare was all right; then Antonia cut the umbilical cord, and they watched in fascination as the little foal staggered to its feet and wobbled to its mother and began to nurse. Antonia grinned, warmth flooding through her. No matter how many times she saw this sight, it never failed to fill her with happiness. She glanced over at Daniel Sutton and saw the same feeling reflected on his face.

Afterward, he directed her to the shower down the central hallway. It was small and spartan, but it was clean, and the water was hot and plentiful, which was enough for Antonia. She had many times made do with much less. Once again clean and dressed in a faded T-shirt and an old pair of jeans, she pushed her feet back into her boots, brushed through her long hair and neatly rebraided it, then made her way to the side door of the farmhouse.

She knocked on the door, then entered when a voice called to come in. Daniel Sutton stood at the kitchen counter in clean jeans and a fresh shirt, his hair slicked back wetly. He was pouring water into the coffee-maker, and he glanced over his shoulder at her as she came in.

''Cup of coffee?'' he asked.

''That sounds nice,'' Antonia replied, feeling a little shy. There was a certain intimacy to the scene—both of them obviously fresh from the shower and him making coffee—that was rather suggestive. She told herself that it was foolish to think that way, but she could not suppress the feeling.

She sat down at the table and glanced around. It was a large, old-fashioned kitchen, but, like the rest of the place, neat and well-kept. She wondered if there was a Mrs. Sutton and was a little surprised to realize that she hoped there was not.

''I was at another Sutton's last week,'' she said, deciding to probe a little. ''Inoculating calves.''

''That'd be my dad, Marshall. Just up the road.'' He nodded in the direction of his father's ranch. ''This was a piece of land I bought from my grandmother.''

''It's nice. You run a good operation, I'd say.''

''Thanks.'' He had finished with the coffee and now stood facing her, leaning back against the counter, arms crossed in front of him.

''Nice house, too. I like your kitchen.''

"Thank you." He glanced around, then shrugged. "James isn't messy. We manage to keep it up okay. It helps not to cook a lot."

Antonia relaxed a little. That statement didn't sound as if there was a woman living here. "James?"

"My son. He's a teenager, but he's a good kid."

Antonia smiled. "You sound as if the two terms are contradictory."

He grinned. "Well..."

"How old is James?" And where is his mother? She could think of no polite way to ask it.

"Eighteen. This is his senior year. He'll be graduating in a few weeks. Next thing you know, he'll be in college." He made a face. "Whew, makes me feel old, saying that."

"You must have married young."

"Straight out of high school. Our parents thought we were stupid, and, of course, we were." He shrugged. "But I guess we all have to make our own mistakes. We split up before James was three."

"I'm sorry."

"Long time ago," he replied briefly, his face shuttered.

There was a long pause. Daniel looked down at the floor, then out the window. Finally he said, "Look. I'm sorry about earlier."

Antonia gazed at him questioningly.

"You know, about wanting Doc Carmichael and all. I was wrong. You did a good job. I—I'm usually not, you know, all chauvinistic and thinking women can't do things. I mean, I guess I am kinda old-fashioned in a lot of ways, but my sister's put me straight any number of times. The thing was, I was worried about my mare.''

''I know.'' Antonia was sure that was true, and she was inclined to give him a second chance. But it didn't seem that she ought to let him off the hook quite yet.

''And I'm not used to women vets,'' he went on. ''I mean, well, actually, I never put much thought to the subject before. I just didn't see how a woman could handle some of the things a horse doctor has to. It's, well, you know, hard work.'' He stopped, color rising in his cheeks. ''Blast, that came out wrong, too. I meant, it takes a lot of physical strength and...''

He trailed off, looking uncomfortable.

Antonia relented. ''Yes. It does. And women don't usually go into a large animal practice because of that. But I've found that horses and cattle are pretty much stronger than men, too. It's all a matter of degree. You just have to compensate for it. I haven't yet had to turn an animal away because I wasn't strong enough.'' She grinned. ''I have to admit, it might be different if I weren't six feet tall. Long arms make a difference.''

He smiled. ''I hope that means you accept my apology. I was wrong. And you did a great job. I hope you'll work on my horses again.''

''I'd be happy to.''

After that, she couldn't think of anything to say, and silence grew uncomfortably. Fortunately, the coffee-maker finished, and Daniel was able to turn his attention to pouring them cups of coffee. He set the cups down on the table and added a carton of milk from the refrigerator and a canister of sugar from the counter.

"Sorry." He cast a rueful eye on the sugar and milk. "I'm afraid we don't have those things..."

"Sugar and creamer?"

"Right." He quirked an eyebrow. "We're kind of plain here. Bachelor household."

"That's okay. I'm kind of plain myself."

"That's hard to believe."

Antonia's eyebrows sailed upward. "What's that supposed to mean?"

He glanced up at her, looking uncomfortable. "Sorry. Have I put my foot in my mouth again? You can see I don't get out much. I didn't mean anything bad. It's just that you look—I don't know, not plain, anyway. You look sort of like Grace Kelly, like some guy in a tux ought to step out onto the veranda and take you back inside to the Harvest Ball."

Antonia chuckled. "Is that a compliment or a put-down?"

"I meant it as a compliment. You're beautiful," he replied simply.

Antonia felt herself blushing. "I...uh..."

"Don't worry. I'm not coming on to you. Just a statement of fact," he said quickly, then sighed. "I'm making a real mess of it, aren't I? James would despair of me if he were here. He thinks I'm the lamest when it comes to women, and he's probably right."

"It's okay," Antonia said with a smile. "I don't mind being told I'm beautiful. It's a lot better than saying I look like a city girl or like I've never gotten my hands dirty in my life, which are also things people have told me." She shrugged her shoulders. "I was cursed with a country club background. I can't even tell people how wrong they are. I was, sorry to say, a debutante."

"Really?" He looked surprised. "You're kidding. I didn't know they had those anymore."

"Oh, yes, still going strong in Richmond, Virginia. It was part of my bargain with my parents—I'd have my coming out if they would let me go to the University of Virginia and get a science degree instead of going to Sweet Briar, like a proper young lady." Antonia was a little surprised at her words. She didn't usually reveal that much of herself to strangers.

Daniel's grin lit up the rugged planes of his face, and Antonia noticed with some surprise that it caused the nerves of her stomach to go into a crazy little dance. It occurred to her that she was feeling about the same age as a debutante.

"Well, I'd say you're about as far as you could get from Sweet Briar now."

"You're right."

"So how you'd wind up in Angel Eye, Texas?"

"I went to veterinary school at Texas A&M," she explained. No need to go into the reasons why she had wound up there. She had found that Texans rarely questioned why anyone would have chosen to come to Texas or to remain once they had lived there a while. They considered that obvious; they were usually curious only about how it had happened. "After that, I wanted to stay in Texas."

Proving her point, Sutton nodded in agreement.

"So I got a job with a vet in Katy." She named a suburb of Houston on the west side of the city. "His practice had a lot of show horse farms, tax write-off cattle places, that kind of thing. I didn't want to live in the city, but I wanted to work with horses, and, well, most large animal vets weren't interested in hiring a woman."

"Chauvinistic pigs," Daniel commented, his black eyes twinkling.

"I know. Terrible, isn't it? Anyway, Dr. Carmichael knew Matt Ventura, the head of the clinic, and he asked him if any of his associates would be interested in moving to Angel Eye and eventually taking over a practice. I was the only one. I wanted to live in the country, and I prefer real working ranches and farms. You know? Where you actually talk to the owner, not some manager hired by a bank president or some cardiologist whose tax lawyer told him to buy a farm for a write-off. Real people who care more about their animals than about how picturesque all the white rail fences look."

"You won't find much of anything picturesque in Angel Eye."

"There's its name," Antonia pointed out. "The Spanish calling it Los Ojos de Los Angeles for the stars."

"And Anglos shortening and anglicizing it," Daniel added. "Yeah, I guess that's pretty unique."

"Angel Eye is real. It has its own unique charm. I like it. Fortunately Dr. Carmichael was getting pretty desperate by that time, so he was willing to take a chance on a woman vet."

"I'm glad." His eyes were warm on her for a moment, reminding Antonia of that moment in the barn when his arms had enfolded her and she had thought about kissing him.

She glanced away from him quickly. "Me too. Well..." She took a last sip of her coffee and stood up. "I'd better be going. I'll be way behind at the clinic."

"I'm sorry."

Antonia shrugged. "It happens all the time. We have emergencies. Dr. Carmichael will have taken up as much of the slack as he can." She hesitated, then said, "It was nice meeting you—well, maybe not nice, but I'm glad we met."

"Me too." He had risen when she did and stood, hands hooked in his back pockets, looking undecided and faintly uncomfortable.

"Thanks for the coffee."

"Any time. I...uh, I reckon the clinic'll just bill me, like they usually do."

Antonia nodded. In a moment, she thought, the two of them would start shuffling their feet and hemming and hawing around like first-graders. Reminding herself that she was a poised, confident adult on a business footing with Daniel Sutton, she stuck out her hand to shake his.

Daniel glanced from her face down to her hand. He reached out and enfolded her hand in his. His was warm and large, the palm roughened by years of calluses. Antonia was startled by the surge of electricity that shot through her at his touch. She raised her eyes to his a little wonderingly, and for a brief moment they looked at each other, unsure, pulses quickening in a way that was a little foreign to both of them.

Then, suddenly, he dropped her hand and stepped forward, his hands going to her shoulders. He pulled her to him, and his mouth swooped down to claim hers.

Chapter 2

Antonia stood stock still, stunned by the sensations that flooded her body. She had dated casually a few times in the four years since Alan, but she had never felt with any of those men the sudden, searing heat that rushed through her now. Her lips beneath Daniel's tingled and burned; her skin was fiercely, instantaneously hot. Her hands came up and curled into the front of his shirt. She trembled; it was as if she were standing on the edge of a precipice, and she wasn't even sure if she wanted to step back or forward.

Just as suddenly, Daniel's mouth left hers. He pulled back and stared down into her eyes, his face mirroring her own confusion. Antonia could feel her blood racing through her veins; she could hear the rasp of her own breath, strained and too fast. Her hands fell away from his shirt. She turned, faintly surprised to find that her legs still worked, and hurried across the room and out the door. By the time she reached the small side stoop, she was running. She dashed across the yard and jumped into the mobile van, never looking back.

She turned the truck around and drove far too fast down the dirt road. As she neared the end of the drive, the electronic gate opened for her. She gunned the engine and rattled out onto the highway. She drove automatically, braking and turning on instinct alone, while her brain tumbled chaotically.

Whatever was she doing—kissing a man she scarcely knew! And a client, at that! And why had it felt so wonderful and scary? Why did she feel as if she might fly apart at any moment?

Her life was calm, even, uneventful. Antonia had worked hard to make it that way, to avoid the chaos that had marked her marriage. Today, in a matter of moments, Daniel Sutton had turned all that hard work upside down. Antonia could not decide whether that more excited, irritated or scared her.

By the time she reached the clinic in town, she had managed to calm her shaking nerves, but she did not have a handle yet on her confused feelings. As she had predicted, her clientele had built up in the waiting room while she was on her emergency call. Almost as soon as she stepped in the back door, Lilian came hurrying down the hall.

"Sorry. We've got a ton of people waiting. Dr. Carmichael tried to take up the slack, but he had a full load this morning. I managed to get a couple of them to just leave their animals, so we could work them in as we can, but you know how most people are. We had one emergency. Doc Carmichael took him.'' She continued to talk as Antonia washed her hands and put on her white lab coat, checking in the small mirror above the sink to make sure that she looked more together than she felt.

Antonia sighed and smoothed down her coat. A lot of work, she thought, would take her mind off her inner turmoil. ''All right,'' she said. ''Let's get to them.''

There was far too great a rush for Antonia to take a lunch break, but finally, around two o'clock, one of the techs who had gone out to eat brought her back a burger, and she gratefully took the bag down to the employee lounge.

The only other person in the lounge was Rita Delgado, one of the technicians and also Antonia's friend. Rita was short, with a voluptuous build, and she was constantly fighting a battle with calories. Today, as was often the case, she was eating a lunch brought from home, consisting of an apple and a carton of nonfat yogurt. Antonia knew that the odds were that Rita would be hitting the snack machines by four o'clock.

Rita glanced up when Antonia entered the room and smiled. ''Hey, come sit down. I haven't seen you all day. What a rush, huh?''

Antonia nodded, going over to the table and setting down her bag. Rita was exactly the person to see if one wanted information. She had a huge circle of family and friends and was always abreast of all the latest gossip. She was also, unfortunately, like a bloodhound once she scented news.

"So..." Antonia sat down in her chair and with studied casualness began to unwrap her burger.

"So?" Rita prodded, eyeing Antonia's sandwich with envy. With a sigh, she dug her spoon into her own cup of fat-free yogurt.

Antonia shrugged. "I don't know. Just a conversation opener."

"What conversation?"

"An awkward one," Antonia admitted, a smile touching her lips as she looked at her technician. "I want to ask you something, but I know you'll go all big-eyed and pushy on me."

"Me?" Rita brought her hand up to her chest dramatically, opening her expressive brown eyes wider, until they looked almost round. "Big-eyed? Pushy? How can you say that?"

Antonia quirked an eyebrow at her. Rita leaned forward.

"So what's the conversation? You can't just throw out a line like that and stop! What's going on?"

"I wanted to ask you a question." Antonia hesitated. "Now, don't read too much into this. I'm only asking out of curiosity."

"Sure. Sure. I know the spiel. Are we talking about a guy here?"

Antonia took a deep breath and plunged in. "Daniel Sutton."

"Daniel Sutton!" Rita sucked in her breath. She stared at Antonia, apparently rendered speechless by Antonia's words.

''Yes, Daniel Sutton,'' Antonia retorted with some asperity. ''Why are you looking at me like that? Is he the local ax murderer or something?''

Rita made a face at her. ''Of course not. He's gorgeous—well, not as gorgeous as Cater. Now, *that* one is the kind that could make a person forget she's a happily married woman.''

''Cater? Who's Cater? What are we talking about here?''

''The Suttons, silly.''

''How many are there? I met his father last week.''

''Oh, there are a bunch of them, all male. Well, except for one sister. Beth. Four boys. They're all gorgeous, even Cory, who's just a baby—he's still in college. Daniel is the oldest, then Cater, then Quinn—he's the sheriff. He's a charmer, too, that one, and there's something about a uniform...'' Rita's voice trailed off dreamily, then she shook herself and went on. ''But he's got that red hair, and I've never been much for redheaded men, myself. Now, my cousin Lena, she's the evening dispatcher over at the sheriff's office, and she says he's sexy as hell. She has the hugest crush on him. But give me a black-haired guy any day, like Cater and Daniel. Cater doesn't live here, though. He's a big writer now, and he lives in Austin.''

''Cater Sutton!'' Antonia straightened. ''The mystery writer? He's Daniel's brother?''

''That's what I just said. I don't read much, but Roberto says he's famous.''

''He is. Definitely. I've read all his books.''

''If you'd rather hold out for him, he comes back

to Angel Eye pretty often. He owns a little house off of Highway 43. Sometimes he stays there for weeks at a time. Roberto says he's recharging his batteries, either that or he comes here to work out the hard parts of his plot. Roberto's got several theories.''

''I am not 'holding out' for Cater Sutton or anybody else,'' Antonia said repressively. ''I was curious about Daniel, that's all. I went to his farm today.''

Rita nodded. ''Lilian told me. How'd it go?''

''I managed to deliver the foal. It was tough, but—''

''I know that.'' Rita grimaced. ''I meant how did it go with Daniel? Is he interested in you? Are you interested in him?''

''I just...wondered what the story was on him. He, uh, well, he was quite obnoxious at first, but then later we talked and—''

''Daniel Sutton?'' Rita asked. ''Obnoxious? Are you serious? Daniel is one of the most laid-back men I've ever met.''

''He wasn't this morning. He was ticked off because I was a woman and he didn't think I could handle his horse.''

''Oh.'' Rita gave a dismissive shake of her head. ''Just worried about his mare, I'll bet. He's a nice man. I've never even heard him raise his voice. He's very quiet, doesn't say much. But I'm guessing what you want to know is whether there is a *Mrs.* Daniel Sutton.''

''Rita...'' Antonia was irritated to feel heat rising in her face. She hated the way her fair blonde's skin gave her away all the time.

Rita chuckled. ''Nothing wrong with that. Who

wouldn't want to know that if they met a hunk like him? Well, there used to be. He married his high school sweetheart is the way the story goes. I'm younger than them, so all I know is hearsay. But what I've heard is that he was crazy as could be about her—Lurleen was her name. Anyway, they got married right after they graduated from high school, and pretty soon they had a kid, James. James is a nice boy. He's friends with my sister Lupe's boy, and I've met him a few times. But Lurleen, they say, couldn't stand life in a little town. She had always wanted to get out, but then she fell for Daniel, so she stayed and married him. Only she still hated it here, and after a while she left town.''

''Oh, no. She left her little boy, too?''

Rita nodded emphatically. ''James was only three years old. Well, you might guess that didn't make her too popular around here. I mean, a husband is one thing, but leaving your own child?''

''So Daniel's raised him alone all these years?''

''Yeah. Did a good job of it, too, from what I've seen. But they say that he still carries a torch for Lurleen.''

''Really? After so long?'' Antonia felt her heart sink a little within her, and she told herself that was foolish.

Rita nodded. ''Yeah. It sounds kinda weird, but that's what folks say.'' She shrugged. ''I don't know if it's true, of course. But what they say is that he never filed for divorce. Finally, after several years, she did.''

''Goodness.''

"'Course, if any guy'd be like that, it'd be Daniel Sutton. He's a solid kind of man...steadfast...loyal."

Antonia thought back to that morning, to the clean, neat farm and house, the obvious care that he had lavished on them, the feeling he had for his horses. She suspected that he was not a very expressive man, but she also would not be surprised to learn that he felt things deeply. She pictured him, a young man alone on that farm with a little boy, doing the best he could for him, always hoping that the woman he loved would return. A pang pierced Antonia's heart.

"That's so sad."

"Yeah." Her assistant cast a sidelong glance at Antonia and added, "I bet the love of a good woman is exactly what he needs. You know, to bring him out of it. I mean, it's been, what fourteen, fifteen years now? He hasn't ever dated much, but you can only carry a torch for so long. You know what I mean? He's bound to be ready to drop it...for the right lady."

"And you're saying that I'm it?" Antonia smiled. "I doubt it."

"Why not? You're a single woman. He's a single man. In a town the size of Angel Eye, there aren't that many opportunities. If it were me, I would jump at a chance like that. Besides, think about all the family reunions—getting to look at all that male pulchritude."

Antonia rolled her eyes. "I don't think so. Number one, I'm not really looking to date anyone. And number two, I don't think a man who's still in love with the wife who deserted him fourteen years ago is the best choice if I were going to date. Men are trouble enough without getting one who's still in love with his ex.''

''Maybe. But a guy like Daniel Sutton—I don't know, he might be worth the extra effort.'' Rita wiggled her eyebrows exaggeratedly.

''How does Roberto put up with you?''

Rita laughed. ''I make it worth his while. Who do you think I do all this suffering for?'' She nodded toward her meager lunch.

''You,'' Antonia retorted, grinning. ''You can't fool me. I heard Roberto last week worrying about how thin you were getting.''

''Oh, that!'' Rita waved away the statement. ''All the Delgado women get to be like bowling balls. He thinks it's normal. But I can tell you he'll notice it when I put on my negligee from Victoria's Secret. But wait—you are *not* going to distract me from the subject of this conversation. Are you interested in Daniel Sutton?''

''I told you, I was curious. It isn't as if he asked me out or anything.'' Antonia wasn't about to tell even a good friend like Rita what had happened that morning at Sutton's ranch.

''Ah, but you'd like him to?''

''I didn't say that.'' Antonia sighed. ''No. I don't want to date him or anyone else. It's too much trouble. I just want to do my work, get settled in Angel Eye....''

''Girl, you've been here two months. How much settling in can you do in a town this size?''

''I'm slow.'' Antonia crumpled up the wrapper from her burger and tossed it in the trash. ''Thanks for the info.'' She paused. ''But if I start hearing about Daniel Sutton from Lilian and the clerk at the Quik-Mart—''

''Antonia...you are so suspicious.'' Rita smiled enigmatically.

''Yeah. Right.'' Antonia gave her friend a knowing look and left the room.

Not surprisingly, Antonia's work spilled over into the evening, and she did not get home until after seven-thirty. She was informed of her tardiness by Mitzi, the black-and-white, tailless street cat that had decided to favor Antonia with her presence last year. The white circle around one eye, in contrast to her mostly black head, gave Mitzi a look of faint surprise, and she carried herself with a feline hauteur that was rather comical, given her bobbed tail, a trait acquired in some accident, Antonia was sure, rather than a genetic anomaly. Mitzi, sublimely unaware of the humorous aspect of her looks, seemed to believe that she was a pampered registered Persian in a wealthy household. She greeted Antonia now with a long litany of complaints, plopping herself down in a seated position in front of the door.

''I hear you, Mitzi,'' Antonia responded. ''Too regal to bother with rubbing my leg, huh?''

She started toward the kitchen, and Mitzi jumped up, bounding forward to get in front of Antonia. Antonia smiled. She was more of a dog lover than a cat person, but Mitzi had been the perfect pet the last few months. Antonia's dog of several years, a beautiful golden retriever named Bailey, had died about six months ago, and Antonia had been unable to bring herself to get another dog, although as a veterinarian she was provided with ample opportunities. Her heart was too bruised by Bailey's death for another loving dog. However, her imperious, distant cat provided the perfect, amusing, faintly aloof companionship she needed.

She dumped out the dry food in Mitzi's bowl, which, having lain there all day, was not fresh enough for Mitzi's refined tastes, and refilled it with food straight from the bag.

"You know," she reminded the cat as she set the bowl down on the floor beside her water, "when I found you, you were rummaging through trash cans for food. How soon we forget."

Antonia knew that she ought to fix herself a nutritious dinner, given the burger that she had grabbed for lunch, but she was too tired, so she dug out one of her large supply of TV dinners from the fridge and put it in the microwave. She had barely sat down at the table with the dinner and a new paperback she had started the day before when the telephone rang. Antonia sighed and took another bite, contemplating not answering it. However, her instincts were too strong, and after two rings she jumped up and snatched the receiver from its cradle.

"Dr. Campbell."

"Antonia, dear. It's Mother."

Antonia suppressed a sigh. "Hello, Mother."

No doubt she was an undutiful daughter, she thought, but conversations with her mother invariably left her angry, depressed, guilty, or all three. It was not a prospect she enjoyed facing at the end of a long, tiring day. She wished sometimes for the warm, friendly relationship she had witnessed between other women and their mothers, but she had finally acknowledged that she would never have that with her own mother. They were simply too dissimilar. She had never been the daughter Elizabeth Campbell wanted, and, frankly, Elizabeth Campbell had never been the mother that Antonia would have chosen if she had been given the chance.

"How are you, dear?" her mother went on in her well-modulated, Tidewater-Virginia voice. "Is everything going well out there?"

"Yes, we're fine out here in the back of beyond," Antonia replied. Her mother had always acted as if her move to Texas had taken her to a foreign country.

"Now, Antonia, I didn't say that."

"Mmm. But that's what you meant."

"I will admit that that Angel place seems an excessively long way away from home. You could have had your practice in Virginia."

"Being a long way from Virginia was the whole point, Mother. It's better all around if I am nowhere near Alan."

"But that was a long time ago, Antonia—almost four years. Don't you think that now you—"

"Mother, we have gone over this before," Antonia pointed out, shoving down her irritation. "I went to A&M because it was far away from Alan, but I like it here. It suits me. Angel Eye suits me."

"Well, of course, dear, if you say so," Elizabeth said doubtfully. "Although I cannot imagine why anyone would name a town such a preposterous name."

"I like the name. It has character. The whole town has character. I feel...good here, relaxed."

"But everyone's foreign—"

"Foreign! Mother, what—"

"I can hardly understand that assistant of yours, that Delgado girl."

"For heaven's sake, Mother, Rita Delgado's lived in Angel Eye all her life. She's no more foreign than you or I. And she hardly even has an accent. I am sure you sound equally strange to her, with those Tidewater 'ou's and dropping all your 'r's."

There was a pause, then Elizabeth went on. "Well, I didn't call to argue."

Antonia bit back the retort that rose to her lips and said mildly, "I don't like to argue, either, Mother. Why don't we just stay off the subject of my moving back to Virginia?"

"All right. I, uh, would you like to hear about the charity auction for the hospital?"

"Sure." Antonia settled down to listen with one ear. She knew that her mother actually did a lot of good with all the energy that she expended on her various society charity projects. However, Antonia found the details of such projects deadly dull. Still, a dull topic was better than an acrimonious one, so she listened, murmuring enough "uh-huh's" and "I see's" to keep her mother going.

Finally Elizabeth paused, then cleared her throat. Now we're getting to the real reason she called, Antonia thought.

"I ran into Alan yesterday. At the club."

Antonia stiffened, her fingers clenching around the receiver. Her chest was suddenly so tight that she could not speak, could scarcely even breathe.

When Antonia said nothing, her mother went on. ''Of course, it was a trifle awkward at first.''

''At first?'' Antonia repeated incredulously. ''Do you mean that then you settled down to a nice conversation with the man who put your daughter in the hospital on more than one occasion?''

''Now, Antonia...don't twist my words. I could hardly cause a scene in the country club. I had to be polite.''

''Naturally.'' Bitterness rose like bile in Antonia's throat. Of course not causing a scene would be the most important thing to her mother.

''I listened to him, that's all. But he, uh, he seemed sincere, Antonia. I think he has changed. He told me he had been to one of those twelve-step things.''

''I'm glad for him, then,'' Antonia retorted coolly.

''He wants to see you, Antonia. He wants to talk to you.''

''Absolutely not!'' Antonia cut across her mother's words. She thought of the odd phone call she had gotten that morning, and a chill ran through her. The events of the day had put the silent caller out of her mind, but now her uneasiness came back in full force. ''You didn't give him my phone number, did you?''

''No, of course not. Really, Antonia...'' Elizabeth hesitated, then said, ''However, I did think that perhaps you ought to listen to him. Give him a chance. He wants to apologize, to set things right with you.''

''I have no need for that.''

''I think he does.''

''Mother, that really doesn't matter to me.''

''He wants to try again.''

''Oh, please.''

"He means it, Antonia. I really think he does. Just think about it. You could have your old life back. You could come home."

"I don't want my old life back!" Antonia snapped. "Can't you understand that? I'm doing what I want, living where I want now. Why do you persist in thinking that I am unhappy or wrong or whatever it is you think just because I don't choose to live your lifestyle? This is what I want. This is what I love."

"But Alan—"

"I don't care about Alan! Frankly, I don't understand why you do. Most mothers would despise any man who did to their daughter what he did to me."

"Of course I detest what he did to you, Antonia. I was merely saying that he has changed."

"Look, I sincerely doubt that Alan has reformed. I cannot tell you how many times he came to me, full of remorse and repentance, crying and begging me to forgive him, promising to make it up to me, promising to stop. They were words, that's all. It never lasted—any more than it would this time if I went back to him."

"But he actually has been working on it. He took a course...."

"One course does not change a lifetime, Mother. But let's give him the benefit of the doubt. Say that he really has changed, that he wouldn't beat me anymore. I still wouldn't marry him again. After all that's happened, after what he did to me, whatever love I felt for him is gone. I could never love him again. Just looking at him would fill me with pain and rage. For his sake, I hope he *has* changed, but his changing will not make *me* feel differently about him. I will never get back together with him, no matter what. If he was asking you to try to soften me, to persuade me to talk to him..."

"He didn't ask me anything like that," Elizabeth retorted stiffly. "He just asked about you—how you were and what you were doing, that sort of thing. Then he told me how much he regretted what had happened, how sorry he was. He didn't try to persuade me to do anything. What I said to you just now—those were my thoughts. I just thought, if he's different, you could..." Her voice trailed off, and she sighed. "You two were such a lovely couple."

Antonia closed her eyes wearily. She reminded herself that her mother was as she was, and there was no changing her at this late date. Appearances mattered to her more than substance. The fact that Alan had been blessed with preppy good looks, excellent manners, and an old and distinguished family, meant far more to her than anything that had been inside him. She would always consider the two of them a lovely couple because they had looked like the country club couple personified: blond, refined, well-dressed. She had considered them perfect for each other because they knew the same people, went to the same parties, had the same backgrounds. She hadn't seen—couldn't see—the anger and pain that had lain beneath the surface.

"Mother...what exactly did he ask you about me? What did you tell him?"

"Oh, just things in general. I did not tell him where you lived, if that's what you mean. He wanted to know if you had finished your studies at A&M and whether you had moved back to Virginia, and of course I said no, that you had decided to stay in Texas. Mostly he wanted to know if you were happy, that sort of thing.''

Antonia frowned. ''How did he know I went to A&M?''

''Well, really, Antonia, how should I know that? It wasn't top secret. I mean, several of our friends knew. Your friends. I'm sure somewhere along the line in the last four years, someone would have told him.''

Antonia worried her lower lip with her teeth. There had been no way to keep her whereabouts completely secret, of course, unless she had completely cut off all ties with her family and friends back home. And just because Alan knew she had been going to A&M didn't mean that he knew anything else about her. Texas was a huge place; he couldn't know that she lived in this small town...except, of course, that over time, her mother would probably mention the peculiar name of the town in talking to her friends, and those people might mention it to someone else, and after a while, just like the information that she was in vet school at A&M, the fact of where she lived would be floating around in the circles in which Alan moved. Circles, she added bitterly to herself, that had obviously not ostracized Alan for committing the small and pardonable sin of abusing his wife.

''Dear, I think you worry too much about whether he knows where you are. I mean, the fact that he knew where you were in school and never bothered you should reassure you, I would think.''

''That's true,'' Antonia admitted. It had been four years since their divorce, and once she had moved away from Virginia, Alan had not tried to see her again. After all this time, he would not go to the trouble of tracking her down, she told herself. There was no reason to think that the caller this morning had been Alan. ''No doubt you are right, Mother. Still, it makes me feel more secure, knowing that he doesn't know where I live.''

''Well, I won't tell him, Antonia,'' Elizabeth said in a patient tone that was guaranteed to set Antonia's teeth on edge. ''Let's talk about something more pleasant. What's going on in your life?''

''I saved a foal's life today, maybe the mother's, too.'' And I met a very handsome man, and he kissed me, and I felt as tingly as a schoolgirl, and I'm not sure what to do about it—if, indeed, there is anything to do.

''That's nice, dear. It sounds quite rewarding.''

''It was.'' Antonia felt guilty. Her mother *was* trying, after all. It wasn't her fault that she didn't understand her daughter. Perhaps she should confide in her mother about Daniel Sutton. Take the initiative to bring about a closer relationship.

At that moment there was a click, and Elizabeth said, with a note of relief in her voice, ''Oh, there's another call. I'm afraid I have to get off, Antonia. Faith Morton is supposed to be calling me with information about the June Gala.''

''Of course. I'm glad you called. Goodbye.''

Antonia hung up the phone and turned back to the table and her supper, no doubt cold by now. She found Mitzi crouched on the table, chowing down on the choicest bits of meat on the tray.

''Mitzi! Oh, well, I'm not hungry anymore anyway.'' Antonia's stomach was alive with nerves now.

Talking about her ex-husband had a way of doing that to her.

She thought about the phone call that morning. It had the markings of one of Alan's calls—jolting her from a sound sleep, the unnerving silence, the hang-up. But then, she reasoned, the same could be said of a dozen other kinds of calls, including a simple wrong number and embarrassed dialer. *There wasn't any reason to believe that it was Alan after all these years.*

Still, she went to the kitchen door and checked its bolt, then continued around the house, checking each window and doorknob. She had forgotten to set the security system—one of her first acquisitions whenever she moved into a new place—and she punched in the keycode now, watching as the reassuring red light began to blink.

She went to the window of the living room, which looked out on the front yard. The blinds were closed, as they always were at night, but Antonia lifted the edge and looked out. The moon was full and cast a bright light across the scene, outlining trees and cars. Nothing moved.

For a long time she stood there, gazing into the darkness, thinking about the past, about how she had gotten here. About Alan.

Chapter 3

Marrying Alan Brent had been the first thing Antonia had done in her life that her mother had approved of wholeheartedly. Antonia had never fit into her parents' country club world, no matter how much her mother had tried to mold her daughter in her own image. The only thing that Antonia enjoyed about her privileged upbringing was the riding. Horses and riding had long been a part of the "aristocratic" Virginia image. She started taking riding lessons when she was seven; riding was even part of the curriculum at the exclusive girls' school she attended. From the moment Antonia was introduced to the huge creatures, she loved them and had no fear of them.

However, even her interest in this one aspect of her life was not enough to reassure her mother, for Antonia did not approach riding as a social activity at which one needed to be competent, but as a passion.

Moreover, she was interested in everything about the animals, not just in learning the proper way to mount and ride. And the one thing concerning horses in which she had no interest was the local hunt club.

Before Antonia finished high school, she knew that she wanted to be a veterinarian and specialize in horses. For that reason she campaigned to go to a respected state university instead of the proper ladies' college that her mother had attended. She had traded making her debut for attending the college she wanted, wading through the tedious balls, parties and teas for the requisite year. After that she had dived headlong into her schoolwork, concentrating on the science courses and academic standing that would get her into veterinary college. It had been her ambition to go to North Carolina State University for her professional training. Then she had met Alan Brent.

It had been during her junior year of college. He had been a senior, blond and blue-eyed, handsome, yet able to blend in with everyone else. She had met him at a fraternity party to which she had reluctantly gone with the son of one of her mother's friends. Her date had gotten so thoroughly drunk that he had passed out under the table in the dining room of the fraternity house, and Alan had politely offered to drive her home. She had been amazed and delighted when he called her the next day and asked her out.

Though she had been told by more than one person that she had blossomed into a beauty, Antonia had never quite gotten rid of the inner feeling that she was the tall gawky wallflower she had been in middle school, when she had spent every tortuous cotillion seated against the wall, waiting for the night to end. Moreover, she was still accustomed to towering over many of the young men she met. Alan, however, was as tall as she, as long as she wore flats, and he was popular, poised and handsome. She was tongue-tied and terribly flattered by his attention, and by their fourth date, Antonia was hopelessly in love with him.

To her amazement, he seemed to be equally in love with her, and by the end of the year, they were engaged. Antonia's mother was almost as delighted as Antonia. Alan Brent's background was as blue-blooded as he appeared to be. The only fly in the ointment, as far as Antonia was concerned, was that Alan was planning to attend Washington and Lee law school. Faced with the prospect of spending the next three years apart from him, she agreed with Alan that the intelligent thing to do was for her to put off her postgraduate plans until he had finished law school. She would get a job while he attended law school, and once he had his degree, they would move to Raleigh so that she could attend vet school.

She sped up her college plans by going to summer school and taking a heavy load the next semester, enabling her to graduate in December. There had been a December wedding, and she had started to work.

Within two months, they had gotten into a fight, which had ended with Alan hitting her and walking out. Antonia, astounded and sick with unhappiness, had cried herself to sleep. The next day Alan had returned, full of remorse and promises. It was the stress of law school, he told her, and it would never happen again. Antonia, eager to believe him, agreed to stay.

That had begun the pattern of their married life. Confused, in love, and steeped in a lifelong habit of guilt for not being the child her parents thought she should be, Antonia had fallen into the classic syndrome of the abused wife. She blamed herself and made excuses for Alan; she hid her bruises and believed each promise that he would change. Living in a new town, she was cut off from her family and friends, and too embarrassed to reveal her problems to any of the people she met at work. They socialized primarily with Alan's classmates, and even if she had felt close enough to any of his friends' wives or girlfriends, she was far too loyal to Alan to reveal him in a bad light to those close to him.

She struggled on, growing more and more isolated, more and more unhappy. Concurrently, Alan's violence escalated. Gradually, she grew to fear and hate him, but she felt trapped, even after they moved back to Richmond. Not surprisingly, when he graduated, Alan had decreed that it was counterproductive to move to Raleigh for Antonia to go to school. He had gotten a splendid offer from a Richmond firm, and, after all, Antonia did not need to get an advanced degree. He would be earning more than enough money for both of them; she wouldn't even have to work anymore if she didn't want to.

Finally, almost two years after they moved to Richmond, Alan had gotten drunk and beaten Antonia up and shoved her down the stairs, giving her a concussion, several cracked ribs and a broken arm. A sympathetic policewoman, unable to get a statement against Alan from Antonia, had given her the name of a psychologist specializing in domestic violence. Four months later, with the help of the psychologist, Antonia had left Alan and filed for divorce.

When she left him, Alan had started a program of harassment that included phone calls at all hours of the day and night, some silent, some filled with verbal abuse, and even more disturbing surprise visits in which he screamed and threatened and pounded on her door. It had culminated, finally, in his breaking into her apartment one night and beating her so badly that neighbors had called the police and Antonia had been taken to the hospital in an ambulance.

As she had lain in the hospital, she had made a vow never to let herself be in a position where such a thing could happen again. When she was released from the hospital, she had gone to her grandmother's house in the Shenandoah Valley. Her grandmother, a faintly eccentric woman who always seemed a trifle surprised that she had produced a son as conservative as Antonia's father, took Antonia in, informing her somewhat gleefully that she had exchanged free rent for her tenant in the cabin up the road from hers in exchange for his protecting her granddaughter. The tenant, a Vietnam vet, had agreed to patrol the road and house after dark; it was, her grandmother pointed out, a great deal for him, as he had trouble sleeping, anyway. The thought of a stranger with a gun roaming around outside in the dark unsettled Antonia at first, but once she had met the quiet, solid man, she had liked him as much as her grandmother did and had been able to get a good night's sleep for the first time since she had gone to the hospital.

While she was recuperating in the mountains, she had applied to Texas A&M veterinary school. She was determined now to have the life she had always wanted, the life interrupted by Alan. North Carolina State, she decided, was too close, and it was somewhere Alan might guess she would go. Texas was far away and not a place where Alan would think of her going. He, like her parents, would assume that she would want to stay on the Eastern Seaboard.

Her grandmother had generously offered to pay for her schooling, and in the fall Antonia had moved to Texas. She had not even told her parents where she was moving, and it was some months before she contacted them in any way except through her grandmother. Finally the nightmares and fears had receded enough that she had told her parents of her whereabouts, but only after their promise to tell no one.

She had known there was the probability of one or the other of them letting slip a reference to her location in a conversation with friends. However, it wasn't too likely that any of them would mention it to Alan, and she hoped that it would take long enough for the information to work its way back in a general way to him that she would already have gotten through with her training and left College Station. When she had moved to Houston and then to Angel Eye, she had tried to impress on her mother yet again how serious and important it was not to reveal where she lived. Her mother swore that she had not told Alan, but obviously, from what her mother had said, Alan had learned through the grapevine that she lived in Texas.

Hopefully that was all he would ever know. *Or*

would ever want to know. Surely by now, she thought, he would have given up his obsession with her. She had not seen or heard from him in four years. Even if he had not straightened himself out, as he had told her mother—and Antonia had grave doubts about the truth of that statement—she could not help but think that he would have moved on. It might rankle that she had gotten away from his control, but it seemed unlikely that he would have strong enough feelings about it that he would go to the trouble of tracking her down this far away.

Still, she could not help but think of that phone call this morning. It had been very much in his style. An involuntary shiver ran down her spine.

No! Antonia clenched her fists. She refused to let the least little thing turn her into a frightened creature again. She had worked long and hard at building a new life for herself. She had defeated Alan and broken his control over her. She had had the courage to leave her family and friends and start all over again in a new place. She was careful, of course—she tried to keep her whereabouts unknown to Alan; she had a security system; she checked her doors and windows; she kept pepper spray in her purse—but those things were part of what helped her not be frightened. She did not leave herself vulnerable to attack, and she was prepared for it if it should happen, so she did not have to be afraid.

She would not let a little thing like a phone call or her mother's talking about Alan make her start cowering under her sheets. She refused to live her life in fear, to worry about Alan and where he was, what he was doing, whether he might show up at any time. To do so would be to give Alan control of her again. That, she promised herself, was the last thing she would ever do. Even if Alan were to find out where she lived and show up here, he would find her very different. He would discover that she could take care of herself, that she was no longer intimidated by him.

She was her own woman now. Antonia turned and walked away from the window.

Daniel Sutton drove by the café a second time, slowing down for a good look. Yes, sure enough, that was the vet's mobile truck in the parking lot of the Moonstone Café.

On impulse, he turned into the next entrance to the parking lot, then stopped, thinking. He had been driving home from the seed store when he had spotted the mobile van, and he had driven two blocks farther before he circled around a few blocks and came back by. Thinking about it, it seemed a little silly and high-schoolish, just as whipping his truck into this lot had been.

First of all, he reminded himself, he didn't even know if Antonia Campbell was in the café. It could have been Doc Carmichael who had been out in the van and had decided to stop in at the café for lunch on his way back. Second of all, he wasn't sure what he would do if Antonia *was* in there. Most likely she had someone with her, one of the technicians or Doc Carmichael or maybe even a client. And if she was alone, what did he plan to do? Just walk up and plop down on the other side of the booth? She would, he felt sure, find him rude and forward. If he went in, he would probably wind up sitting down and eating at some other table and watching her—unless, of course, she finished eating and left as he came in. That would be just his luck.

Daniel knew that he had never been much good at dating. He and Lurleen had gone steady from the beginning of their junior year. Before that he had had a few dates with Suzette Carpenter, who had been visiting her grandmother in Angel Eye the summer after his sophomore year. Looking back on it, though, he realized that Suzette, a year older and way more sophisticated than he, had more or less maneuvered him into asking her out. And he had known Lurleen since they were kids. It wasn't like dating a stranger.

He had gone out some since his divorce, had even had one or two fairly long relationships, but he knew that he was a novice in the field of dating, and he always found the process awkward, especially in the initial stages. This time, however, it was even worse. He felt like he was back in high school, he was so full of nerves and doubts.

He could hardly remember the last time he had had this sort of reaction to a woman. When he walked out of the barn the other morning and saw her, he had felt as if someone had slammed him in the gut. It had been a surprise, of course, expecting Doc Carmichael and instead seeing a gorgeous blonde. But it hadn't been only surprise. It had been the immediate, unmistakable kick of sheer lust.

She had looked pristine and untouchable, a Society girl with ice in her veins but a face so lovely it made his heart clench, and mile-long legs that drove everything from his mind but the thought of having them wrapped around him.

It had been unnerving. He was still unnerved. That was, he thought, one reason why he had gotten so angry at her presence. He was a man who prided himself on his calm and control. He liked his life on an even keel, without all the emotional turmoil that had marked it with Lurleen—the bursts of passion, the long, dark nights of pain, the worry and doubt. All that was far in the past, and he had found that it was much easier to live this way. He dated women he liked, but he never fell head over heels in love with them. He didn't lose control, didn't get carried away.

So to feel such an electric shot of longing was not only unexpected but also faintly frightening, and he had reacted with a swift surge of anger.

It still bothered him. He didn't like the fact that he had been unable to get Antonia Campbell out of his mind. He didn't like the way his thoughts kept lingering over that kiss as she left. Most of all, he didn't like the fact that when he saw her mobile truck parked in the café parking lot, his heart had skipped a beat and he had been compelled to return.

On the other hand, he couldn't remember the last time he had felt this excited, eager and alive, either. It probably was foolish. He had decided long ago that most things connected with love were foolish. It was also, apparently, something he could not control with his usual ease. In fact, he found himself not wanting to control it.

It was kind of nice, in a way, to feel like a kid with raging hormones again.

Daniel opened the door of his truck and stepped out, reminding himself that it was even more foolish to sit out here in the parking lot, doing nothing. He walked across the asphalt and went in the front door.

Daniel paused inside the door and looked around the room. It was a typical lunchtime crowd; practically every table and most of the stools at the counter were full, and the air was vibrating with the noise of people talking. The Moonstone Café was a bit out of place in Angel Eye. It had been started three years ago by Jocelyn Kramer, a willowy woman with dark, wildly curling black hair, who had moved here from Dallas, seeking, according to the gossips, to get away from the big city. There were all sorts of rumors about why, ranging across everything from marital troubles to a nervous breakdown to some sort of New Age strangeness. But whatever had impelled her to come, she was a hell of a good cook, and her small restaurant had flourished.

For a moment it all seemed a blur of faces. Then Daniel spotted Antonia, sitting by herself in a booth in the back, a glass of iced tea and an open book in front of her. His stomach knotted. This was the moment of decision. He had to do it now. In another minute one of the waitresses would turn and see him and come lead him to a seat, and he knew that he would not have the nerve to tell her that he would rather sit with Antonia.

Swallowing hard, he started threading his way through the tables, nodding to people he knew. He stopped to talk to two of his father's friends whom he knew would be offended if he didn't. By the time he drew near Antonia's table, she had looked up from her book and was watching him approach.

He had been rehearsing what he would say all the way across the room, but once he saw her eyes on him, all thoughts went straight out of his head. Daniel reached her table and stopped. His mouth went dry, and he couldn't think of a thing to say.

"Hi," Antonia said after a moment. "How are you?"

Daniel was too busy with his own problems to notice that her voice had a slight tremor to it. Antonia, however, heard it and felt like slapping herself. *Why did she always seem to turn to quivering jelly around this man?*

She had spent a great deal more time than was wise the past two days thinking about Daniel Sutton and had even considered calling to ask about his mare and foal just to have a chance to talk to him. In other circumstances, she probably would have called to make sure that everything was going all right, but because it was him, she knew that the call would be as much excuse as concern. *What if he saw through it? What if he assumed that she was calling because of that kiss?*

So she had not called, but still she had found her mind wandering all too often to the subject of whether and how she would see him again. When she had looked up just now and seen him walking through the dining room, pausing to chat to various friends, her heart had slammed into overdrive. He seemed to be coming straight toward her, and that fact made it even more difficult to breathe. She was surprised that she was able to squeeze out a hello.

"Hi," Daniel returned, jamming his hands in the front pockets of his jeans. "Nice to see you."

"Yeah. I mean, it's nice to see you, too. How is your mare?"

"Great. She's doing real well. The foal, too."

"That's good."

They both nodded, and Daniel glanced around the restaurant. "Kinda crowded today. 'Course, I guess it always is."

"It has been every time I've been here." Antonia groaned inside at the lameness of her conversation, but she could think of nothing to say. She wondered if any other thirty-year-old woman was this tongue-tied around a man. *You'd think she had never dated.* Not, of course, she added silently, that she was dating Daniel. *Far from it.*

As he cast another glance around them, it occurred to Antonia that he was perhaps hinting for an invitation to join her. "Would you—I mean, why don't you sit here? Since it's so crowded."

"Okay," he answered with alacrity and slid into the seat across the booth from her. He let out a long sigh. "Well...I don't feel *too* stupid."

"Why? What are you talking about?"

"Ah, hell, I wanted to come sit down here as soon as I walked in the door. Then, when I got here, I stood around like a teenager. No, worse, a ten-year-old. I'm sure James is much suaver than I am."

Antonia grinned. "Well, if it helps you any, I'm

equally inept. Maybe we're too used to working with animals instead of people.''

He smiled back at her. ''That may be the case with you, but I'm afraid I've always been that way. Many was the time that Cater about despaired of me. He always had more dates than me, and he was a year younger.''

''Your brother?''

Daniel nodded. ''Yeah. The whole crew's pretty good at talking, except for me. I took after my Dad. The rest were like Mama.''

''I met your father. You're right. He isn't much of a talker. But I liked him right off.''

''Yeah. He's a good guy. Old-fashioned and all.''

''Hey, Daniel.'' A middle-aged woman with improbably bright red hair stopped by their table, order pad in hand. ''You sittin' here?''

''Hi, Marlene. Yeah. I thought I would. Pretty crowded today.''

''Un-huh.'' Marlene smiled—a little too broadly, in Daniel's opinion. Her gaze flickered to Antonia and back to him. ''Know what you want?''

''Sure. The, uh, chicken-fried steak, I guess.'' Daniel hadn't in fact glanced at the menu, so he named a dish they were sure to have. No café in Angel Eye could have been successful without serving it. ''Iced tea.''

''Sure thing.'' Marlene slipped the order pad into the pocket of her apron, glanced again at Antonia and walked away.

Daniel sighed, watching her go toward the kitchen,

and turned back to Antonia. "I guess this will be all over town by nightfall. Sorry."

"What? What will be all over town?"

"That we had lunch together. Except that by five this afternoon they'll probably have us engaged."

Antonia's eyebrows rose. "Just because we ate at the same table?"

"Little town, ma'am. Not much to do besides gossip, and everybody knows everybody—their family, their history, oh, hell, just everything." His mouth quirked up in a smile, and he shot her a quizzical look. "Don't tell me someone hasn't already told you that I'm divorced with an eighteen-year-old son, and that I have three brothers and—"

"One sister," Antonia finished, chuckling. "Yes. Rita Delgado filled me in."

"That's what I'm saying. Everyone knows everything. It's hard to keep a secret. But what's worse is that they speculate and embellish until the rumors hardly resemble what really happened." He paused, then added, "Just wait. You'll see what I'm talking about. Bachelors tend to stir up a great deal of curiosity, I've found. 'Course, newcomers are topics of great interest, as well. Put the two together..."

"But it must not bother you that much. You still live here."

"Sure. Wouldn't live anywhere else. The thought of living in someplace like Dallas or Houston is enough to give me the heebie-jeebies. Cater is always going on about all the things there are to do in Austin and all that. But I figure, if it's so great there, how come he bought a house here and comes back all the time?''

Antonia smiled. ''It's a nice town. I like it.''

''So you reckon you'll stay?''

Antonia nodded. ''Yeah. As long as the horsemen and ranchers don't rebel against having a woman vet.''

''Now what kind of fool would object to a woman vet?'' he asked, his eyes alight with humor. ''I doubt there's anybody like that around here.''

''A few,'' Antonia retorted.

''I guess everybody can't be as forward thinking and tolerant as I am.''

''Yeah. Too bad, isn't it?''

The waitress came up to their table with Daniel's glass of iced tea. After she set it down, she lingered to straighten a chair at the table closest to them and rearrange the sugar packets. Daniel glanced back at her, then cast a meaningful look at Antonia. She grinned. It was obvious that the waitress was hoping to hear some of their conversation.

The two of them said nothing as Daniel put sugar and lemon in his tea and stirred it. After a few moments Marlene gave up and went off to wait on another customer.

After she left, they continued to sit in silence until it began to stretch out awkwardly. Antonia cast about for something to say and came up blank. *Why was it that this man made her feel tongue-tied and foolish, like a schoolgirl again?* Daniel shifted in his seat.

''So tell me,'' he said finally. ''I understand why you came to Angel Eye and all, but how did a debutante wind up becoming a vet?''

''Horses,'' Antonia answered succinctly. ''Riding is still a First Family of Virginia sort of thing to do. The school that I went to even had a stable, and riding lessons were part of the curriculum. English saddle, of course. Well, it was the one thing about that sort of life that I loved. I was crazy about horses from the minute they put me on one's back. I was one of those stereotypically horse-mad adolescent girls. I must have read the Walter Farley books a million times. I collected horse figurines. I watched *National Velvet* every time it came on TV. At school I spent all my spare time down at the stables. I would follow the vet around whenever he came and absolutely plague him with questions. Finally he let me come down to his clinic to watch him work for a career day thing we did in middle school. From then on I was hooked. 'Course, my mother nearly fainted when I announced at sixteen that I wanted to go to veterinary school.'' She quirked an eyebrow. ''Not exactly a career for a proper young lady.''

''What did she want you to do?''

''Hmm. I'm not sure. Follow in her footsteps, I guess—go to a 'good' school socially and marry well, then keep all the charities in the greater Richmond area in business.''

''That's what she does? Charity work?''

Antonia nodded. ''I suppose it really is a career. Worthwhile, too. But it can't compare to saving an animal's life. She never could understand that. All she could see was the mess and blood and plebeian-ness of it. My mother and I are poles apart.''

''Happens sometimes.'' Daniel looked suddenly so-ber. "I guess that's the way it is with James and me. He has about as much interest in raising horses as I do in nuclear physics. All he's interested in is films. He wants to go to the film school at UT and then go to Los Angeles." His face turned both pained and puzzled. "L.A.," he repeated, shaking his head.

Antonia chuckled. "You make it sound like the other side of the moon."

He smiled self-deprecatingly. "Have to admit, it kinda seems that way to me. I'd like to blame it on Jackson," he went on wryly, "but I can't. James was crazy about movies before he came along."

"Jackson? Who's Jackson?"

"Jackson Prescott. My sister's husband. Don't tell me that Rita left that out?"

"She said you had a sister, but she didn't say anything about her husband. Why? Does he have something to do with movies?"

Daniel's grin spread. "I knew there was something about you I liked. I didn't know who he was, either. James acted like I had spent my life in a cave. He's some big Hollywood producer guy. My sister met him when he was out here scouting locations for a movie he was making. We wound up in one of those tabloids—the whole family."

"A tabloid?" Antonia's eyebrows rose. "I can't believe Rita didn't tell me."

"Me neither. It was a hot topic around here for a few months."

"How did you wind up in a tabloid?"

Daniel shifted in his seat. "Damn! Why was I fool enough to bring this up?"

"Come on, you can't squirm out of this. You have to tell me what happened. You can't drop something like that in my lap and then not explain it."

"Well, the truth was—I hit him."

"You hit him? You mean, like, knocked him out?"

"No. It wasn't that bad. The hospital blew it all out of proportion."

"The hospital? You mean you had a fist fight with this guy in a hospital?" Laughter bubbled up Antonia's throat.

"Well...yeah." Daniel had to chuckle. "Sounds like I'm a heller, doesn't it? Truth is, I hadn't hit anybody in probably fifteen years. I was steamed. I thought he was somebody else—the guy that got my sister pregnant and dumped her. There she was—alone and pregnant, going to have to raise the baby by herself—because while this slick guy was getting her to fall for him, he forgot to mention the minor detail that he was already married. I hated the very thought of the guy. Anyway, she went into labor, and nobody was there with her. The hospital called us, and we went rushing over. We were pretty worried."

"We? You and your dad?"

"Yeah. And Quinn and Cory. He was home from college at the time."

Antonia smiled, a picture forming in her mind of the four Sutton men storming into the hospital.

"And there Jackson was, cool as you please, looking like he had every right to be there. The nurse said he was the baby's father."

"So you punched him."

"Yeah," Daniel admitted somewhat shamefacedly.

"I'm usually not so impulsive. But Beth's my baby sister...."

"I think it's kinda sweet, actually."

"Yeah, right. Kinda stupid, really. I felt like ten times an idiot when Beth told me then that he was a total stranger who had kindly stopped to help her when she went into labor on the side of the road." He began to chuckle, remembering. "Then James came in, and when he heard who the guy was, he about had a coronary. Seems he was a famous director and producer."

"And this made all the papers?"

"Oh, yeah. It was a real mess. They were saying that Joseph was his 'secret love child,' that kind of stuff. The fight just made it a little juicier."

"I bet. Wow. I'm sorry I missed all this."

"Sounds better than it was, believe me."

"I'm sure." Antonia chuckled.

She couldn't remember when she had felt this at ease and relaxed with a man. She had dated since her marriage, of course; she had more or less forced herself to after a couple of years had passed and she had realized that she had sealed herself off almost completely from men. She was determined that she would not let Alan rule her life in any way. However, many of those times had felt exactly like being forced, and it was rare that she really let down her defenses and enjoyed a date. As a result, she had gone out with very few men more than a few times.

But somehow this quiet man had sneaked in past her walls and shaken her careful reserve. The past few days she had felt a number of things regarding him that she was not used to experiencing anymore, and it was a little unsettling. It was also exciting.

They continued to talk until their lunches came, meandering from topic to topic. With the arrival of their meals, their conversation died down, and for a few minutes they concentrated on the delicious food on the table before them.

When she finished eating, Antonia set her fork down with a contented sigh, saying, "That's one of the things I really like about Angel Eye."

"What? This café?"

"Yes. It's unusual for a small town."

Daniel grinned. "You mean you didn't know that Angel Eye is a center for haute cuisine?"

Antonia responded with a pointedly arched eyebrow and a nod toward the remains of his chicken-fried steak dinner.

"Well, maybe not haute," he admitted. "But really good. Thank heavens Jocelyn decided to move here. Sure beats the truck stop on Highway 43."

"Tell me about it. I've eaten there." Antonia paused, realizing with a distinct sense of disappointment that now that the meal was over, she would have to leave. It took her aback somewhat to know how little she wanted to go. "Well..." She proffered a small smile. "I better return to the clinic."

"Yeah." Daniel stood up as she did. "I—uh—"

"It was nice seeing you again," Antonia said, unconsciously slipping back into her usual formality.

"Yes. I—I was thinking—you don't keep any horses, do you?"

"No. I live in town. Someday I hope to get a bigger place and be able to have a horse."

"Well, if you want to ride, you're welcome to at my place."

"Really?" The eagerness that rose in her was only partly due to the thought of getting to ride again, Antonia knew. "That's very kind of you. I would like to, if you're sure it's all right."

"More than all right." His dark eyes turned warmer in a way that made Antonia's pulse beat a little faster. "I would really like it. This Saturday, maybe?"

"That would be nice. I'll be there. Say ten or so?"

He nodded. "Sure."

"Thank you." Antonia hesitated, feeling a trifle awkward, then put out her hand to shake.

Daniel took it, his larger hand curling around hers. His palm was callused and warm, and the touch of it sent an electric thrill up Antonia's arm. She couldn't help thinking of the way he had kissed her when she left his house the other day, and heat rose in her cheeks. She was suddenly very aware of the eyes of the other diners on them. She pulled her hand back out of his grasp, offering him a slightly shaky smile.

"See you." She turned and walked toward the front of the café. She wondered if Daniel was watching her leave. She didn't dare turn around to see, with everyone in the café watching them like hawks. Saturday, she thought, and couldn't keep a smile from forming on her lips. *Saturday.*

Chapter 4

Antonia thought a dozen times of calling Daniel and telling him that she could not come ride on Saturday. It was foolish to get involved with one of her clients. *Foolish, really, to date anyone from a small town like this.* Daniel had been right. By the time she got back to the clinic after their lunch, everyone there had known about them eating together at the Moonstone Café. There were no secrets in Angel Eye, apparently, and that meant that everyone she knew would be monitoring their relationship. If they dated for a while, people would be bugging her about when they were going to get married. And if they broke up, then everyone would be pumping her for the details about that. Besides, in a town this size, she was bound to run into Daniel sometimes, and that would be awkward once they were through dating.

And it *would* end in a breakup of some kind, she

was sure. Antonia had no intention of marrying again; she wanted no relationship other than a casual one. But a relationship could not stay casual forever—not with the sort of sizzle she felt when she kissed Daniel. They would either lose interest or the dating would escalate, and that would inevitably lead to a stormy breakup when they reached the point she would not go beyond. It would be better never to let it develop at all, she pointed out to herself reasonably.

But every time she started toward the telephone to call him, she hesitated. After all, going out to Daniel's place to ride horses one morning did not mean they were having a relationship. It didn't really qualify as a *date.* And if he asked her out on a real date, she could always refuse. Besides, she *wanted* to go. She wanted to ride again. She wanted to see Daniel.

In the end, she did nothing, which meant that Saturday morning she drove out to Daniel's farm. She was once more in jeans and boots, but this time she had put on more makeup, and she wore a more attractive blouse than the plain, mannish kind of shirt she usually wore to work.

She knocked on the kitchen door, for in Angel Eye, it was still more the customary country entrance than the formal front door. A moment later the door was opened by a tall, dark-haired teenager. He was gaunt in the way of teenage boys whose height has outstripped the rest of their growth, with cheekbones so sharp they looked as if they could cut paper, intense dark eyes, and a full, sensitive mouth. He was, Antonia suspected, the object of most of the area girls' adolescent crushes, for he looked the epitome of the sullenly handsome teenage hunk.

He smiled, dispelling the sullen image, but making Antonia adjust her estimation of his crush quotient even higher.

"Hi. You must be James."

"Yeah." He looked at her curiously, but opened the screen door for her. "Come in. You, uh, you here to see my dad?"

"Yes." Antonia smiled. "He didn't tell you I was coming? I'm Antonia Campbell. The new veterinarian."

"Oh! Yeah, he told me the new vet was coming. He didn't say you were a knockout. Heck, he didn't even say you were a woman."

"Perhaps it slipped his mind."

"I doubt that," James replied with an admiration so apparent that it boosted Antonia's spirits. "Come on in and sit down." He led her through the kitchen into the family room beyond. "You want some coffee? Dad's down at the barn. He said he'd be right back."

"That sounds nice. Thank you."

James went back into the kitchen. Antonia glanced around the family room. It was an obviously masculine lair, large and a little untidy, furnished with a well-worn leather couch and two leather recliners. A saddle sat in one corner, and several issues of some horse-oriented publication were scattered across the coffee table, along with a trigonometry text and an entertainment magazine. There was a fireplace in the center of one wall and a dark wood mantel above it. Several photographs in frames stood on the mantel, and Antonia walked over to look at them. There were pictures of various men in groups and alone, as well as a picture of a lively looking woman with red, curling hair, and one of an attractive blond woman. The same blonde was in another portrait, this one hanging on the wall beside the fireplace, in which she sat holding a baby in her lap.

James came back into the room, two mugs in his hands. "Looking at our rogues' gallery? That's mostly Dad's family." He came across the room to hand her one of the mugs. "I didn't think to ask. Do you want sugar or milk? I can go back and get them."

"No, black is fine."

"That's my Uncle Quinn there in the cop uniform. That's when he was with the police in San Antonio. And this is Dad's sister, Beth. That's me and my friend, Dolan, last year after the district championship game."

Antonia's eyes went involuntarily toward the portrait of the blond woman with the child on the wall. James looked embarrassed. "That's me and my mom when I was a year old. I look like an idiot."

"You look very nice," Antonia corrected. "You were a handsome baby."

He grimaced. "But check out that sailor suit they put me in. That's just cruel."

Antonia chuckled and turned back toward the couch. She had suspected that the woman was Daniel's ex-wife. *But who kept pictures of their ex around?* She remembered Rita's statement that everyone thought Daniel still carried a torch for his ex-wife. These pictures sitting in his living room seemed to support that argument. Not, of course, she reminded herself, that it made any difference to her. She barely knew the man.

James followed, sitting down in the chair beside the couch. His dark eyes were alight with curiosity. "So…when did you meet Dad?"

"A few days ago. One of his mares had a problem delivering."

"Oh. Yeah, I remember him saying that," James admitted. "But he didn't mention you."

"Well, he mentioned you to me."

"Really?" The young man looked wary. "What'd he say?"

Antonia chuckled. "Actually, he said that you were a good kid, I believe. Said you want to be a director."

"Yeah. I'm surprised he admitted it, though. I think he's hoping that if he ignores it, it'll go away."

"That's a better approach than some. My mother used to argue with me endlessly."

"Dad's done some of that, too." His grin indicated that he didn't take such arguments particularly seriously. "So your parents didn't want you to be a vet? How come?"

"They didn't consider it an appropriate occupation for a lady."

"Really?" His eyebrows rose expressively. "I didn't know people still said things like that."

"My parents live somewhat in the past."

"At least Dad doesn't say stuff like that. But I can tell he's disappointed in me. He keeps telling me how iffy the movie business is." He made a face. "Like raising cattle or horses isn't risky?"

"You have a point there," Antonia agreed. "But,

you know how it is—*the devil you know* and all that..."

"I guess. Mostly I think he feels like I'm deserting him," he said astutely. He shrugged, looking troubled. "I mean, it's always been just him and me. My mother left a long time ago. So it was always kind of us against the world or whatever. I think he figured I'd go into ranching, too. Take over the place and all that."

"Could be."

"But it doesn't have anything to do with him. I just...this isn't what I want to do. It's boring. You know?"

Antonia smiled. "I'm probably the wrong person to ask. I find animals interesting."

"Oh. Well, yeah, I guess you would. I don't, though. Movies are what I like. I mean, I know it's a hard business to break into and all that, and it's real easy to fail. But what am I supposed to do? Not try it just because I might fail?"

"No. I'm sure he doesn't mean that."

"I guess." He paused, then cast her a rueful smile. "Sorry. You probably didn't come here to hear about the Sutton family wars."

"I don't mind."

"You're easy to talk to. I don't usually dump that on people when I first meet them."

"It's okay. Really."

A silence fell on them. Antonia looked down at her cup of coffee. She could feel the boy's eyes on her curiously. *Probably wondering why she was here...if she had designs on his father.* She had to admit, she rather wondered the same thing.

"You're a senior this year?" she asked, grasping at conversational straws.

He nodded, and at that moment there was the sound of boot heels on the kitchen floor, and a moment later Daniel hurried into the room. His eyes went immediately to Antonia.

"Hey, Doc." His slow smile illuminated his face, and Antonia felt herself melting a little into the couch.

"Hi."

"Sorry I wasn't here when you arrived. I was checking on the horses."

He, too, was dressed in the usual jeans and shirt, but the warm browns of his shirt did nice things for his eyes, and Antonia could frankly not imagine anything that better suited the long, muscled line of his legs than his faded denim trousers, worn to a buttery softness. He was freshly shaved, and his hair was still damp from the shower, and he smelled faintly of a masculine cologne. All in all, Antonia thought, the sight of him did funny things to her nerves.

"It was no problem," she assured him. "James has been good company."

Daniel turned faintly wary eyes on his son, as if he wasn't sure whether she was joking.

"What?" James asked, a frown marring his handsome face. "We just talked."

Daniel's jaw set. "I didn't say anything."

"Yeah. Right." James rolled his eyes and rose to his feet. "Nice to meet you, Ms.—I mean, Dr.—Campbell."

"It was nice meeting you," Antonia responded as the boy left the room. *Obviously these two had not exactly mastered the art of communicating.*

Daniel's eyes followed his son out of the room, then he turned back to Antonia. "Well, you ready for a ride?"

"Sounds lovely."

Antonia finished off her coffee and set the cup in the sink, and they started out the door toward the stables.

"I meant it, you know," she told him as they walked across the yard. A black-and-white dog loped toward them happily, tongue lolling from its mouth, and raced around them in circles. "James was quite nice, and we had a pleasant conversation."

"Good." Daniel looked visibly relieved as he reached down to pet the dog. "He's always been polite enough, but sometimes I'm not sure what he's going to do. When he was little, I always knew what to expect. We were real close. But the last few years..." He shook his head. "Sometimes I feel like I don't know him anymore."

"Yeah, he said that it had always been the two of you against the world."

"Really?" Daniel cast her a surprised glance. "He said that?"

Antonia nodded. "Yes. He seemed quite fond of you. Worried about upsetting you."

He looked even more astonished. "James said that?"

Antonia shrugged. "Not in so many words, but, basically, yeah, that was his concern. He feels you're disappointed in him because he doesn't want to take over your business."

"Disappointed!" Daniel frowned. "I'm not disappointed. I mean, well, I am disappointed that he won't be here, that he won't be working with me. But I'm not disappointed in *him.*"

"I didn't think you were. But it might help if you told him that."

He cast her a sideways glance. "Straight out like that?"

Antonia chuckled. "Yeah. I know it's hard for you strong, silent types, but saying stuff 'straight out like that' can make for a more comfortable relationship."

"You think?" He looked decidedly *un*comfortable at the thought. "It's sure different from when I was growing up. My dad and I never—I mean, we talked, but not about things like that."

"Feelings and such?"

"Yeah." He gave her a lopsided grin. "Guess I sound like a relic, huh?"

"Maybe. A little." Her smile took the sting out of the words. "But there are some nice things about being old-fashioned."

"Yeah? Like what?"

"Well, you raised a nice, polite, thoughtful boy who loves and respects you. That's good, isn't it?"

"Yeah. James is a good kid. I'm not sure that I can take the credit for that, though."

"No doubt he had good genes. But I suspect a big portion of the credit goes to you. You are the one who raised him. That's a big task—bringing up a child without a mother."

"Yeah. My youngest brother Cory pretty much grew up without a mom, too. She died when he was a little kid. But at least he had Beth—my sister. She was a teenager when she died and kind of a little mother to him." He went on thoughtfully. "Come to think of it, I guess we always had my mother or Beth there to interpret." He grinned at her. "You know, tell us what we were all feeling. 'Dad's so proud of you for winning the blue ribbon at the county fat stock show.' 'Cory's hurt that you didn't look at his plastic brick tower.' Probably James and I could have used some of that."

"Probably."

He cocked an eyebrow. "Care to come over and translate for us every so often?"

Antonia smiled. "I think you two can handle it."

"I don't know. You may be giving us too much credit."

They had reached the corral beside the barn, where Daniel had already bridled and tied two horses. One was a sorrel gelding with a white blaze down his face, and the other was a black mare. Two pairs of ears twitched forward, and the horses regarded Antonia with interest. While Daniel went into the barn for the saddles, Antonia made friends with them, talking in a low, melodic voice and reaching out to stroke their necks. The black-and-white dog sat down beside her, tail thumping the ground. Antonia reached down to scratch him behind his ears.

"You ready to go for a run, too, fella?" she asked.

"Beautiful horses," she commented to Daniel as he

put a blanket and saddle on the sorrel. "You obviously take good care of your animals."

"Thank you. I try. The mare's Alabama. She's lively but gentle. Tambor's strong and fast, but he's got this gait that'll jar your teeth out of your head. I figured not your first time out."

"Sounds like a wise choice. And Alabama looks absolutely beautiful to me. Here. I can do that," she added as Daniel swung a saddle onto Alabama's back.

"Sure?" Daniel stepped back. "You're my guest."

"Ah, but not, I hope, a *bothersome* one," Antonia retorted. "I intend to get invited back."

Daniel smiled, his dark eyes lighting with warmth. "I wouldn't worry about that."

Antonia felt heat rising in her cheeks. "I—I'm sorry. I wasn't really angling for another invitation. I was just…talking. You must think me terribly rude."

"Not at all," he assured her. "I'm glad you would like to come back." His gaze flickered down to her mouth for an instant before he added teasingly, "Even if it is just the horses you want to come for."

"Daniel!" Antonia started to protest but realized that she would just be digging herself in deeper if she went on. Instead, she contented herself with shooting him a look, then set to the task of buckling on her saddle.

Her hands moved quickly and expertly, with years of practice. She concentrated on the job, aware that Daniel was covertly watching her. Even though she was a veterinarian, she knew that he would not be completely certain of her ability to saddle and ride a horse until he had watched her. The fact did not upset her; she, too, would have to see a person's competence before she would trust him with a horse, no matter how much of an expert he claimed to be.

They led the horses out of the corral, mounted and rode eastward, the dog, whose name she had found out was Solo, trotting happily at their side. Antonia let out a sigh of pure pleasure at being on a horse again. It had been at least three months since she had ridden, and even before that, she had not ridden as much during the year she had worked in Houston as she was accustomed to.

Alabama was, as Daniel had promised, biddable, but quick and energetic, as well. Antonia concentrated on getting acquainted with her and with riding again. Daniel rode alongside her in comfortable silence.

Antonia looked over at him and smiled. "This is wonderful! Thank you so much for inviting me."

"Any time," he replied. "I enjoy the company. I thought we'd ride over to the mesa." He pointed to the flat-topped upthrust of land rising off to their right. "There's a little creek there, and some shade."

Antonia turned her horse's head in the direction he indicated. They rode along through the sparse vegetation, winding through feathery-leafed mesquite bushes, sagebrush and spiny prickly pear cacti. Now and then a yucca plant raised a long stem upward, adorned at the top with a cluster of white bells. It was different seeing the land close up like this, Antonia thought, instead of viewing it through the window of her truck as she sped along the highway. She could feel herself relaxing, lulled by the rhythm of the horse and the heat of the sun shining down on them. A breeze rustled the leaves of the bushes and lifted her hair, caressing her cheek. It wouldn't be hard to be content out here, she mused, not when one could always saddle a horse and ride one's cares away.

She glanced over at her companion. It was no wonder that Daniel exuded such strength and calm. He had grown up like this, riding the land with his dog by his side, surrounded by the love of animals and the beauty of nature. It was, she thought, one of the best things anyone could give a child. No wonder he found it hard to understand why his son, given the same upbringing, wanted other things.

"It must have been wonderful growing up here," she told him.

He smiled. "I didn't always think so, particularly when I had to get up at five o'clock to do my chores before the school bus came. But, yeah, I wouldn't trade it for anything. I never wanted to live anywhere else." He grinned. "Little different from Virginia, though, I guess."

"Yeah. But it's beautiful, too, in its own way. I like the land out here." She gazed out over the rugged landscape. "But you have to wonder what people thought when they moved here, years and years ago. So different from home, so empty and vast."

"A bunch of 'em probably turned right around and went back. That'd be my guess. The rest of them just saw opportunity. My great-great-grandfather came out here after the Civil War. They had five kids. Only two of them lived to be adults. His wife died in childbirth. His brother came out with him, but he wound up going back to Alabama. There've been Suttons here ever since. Dad's land is just over there. Mine abuts it. This was my grandmother's land. She and her sisters divided her father's ranch when he died. It's not big enough for running cattle, really, but it's enough for my horse farm."

"You've done a good job with it."

"I've tried. But sometimes I wonder if I did the right thing. Maybe I was selfish, staying here. James's mother hated it. Now he wants to leave, too. Maybe they would have been happier in the city."

"No. Don't think that way. Maybe James does want to live somewhere else, do something else, but he will always carry this with him. I'm sure he's better and stronger for having the kind of life he had here. What about your brothers and sister? They don't live here, do they? But it's part of them."

"Yeah. Cater bought a house here and a little piece of land. He comes back a lot. Says he can think better here. And when Beth had problems, she came back to the ranch." He looked at her and smiled. "You have a real knack for that, you know."

"For what?"

"Making me feel better."

The warmth in his eyes sent a funny flutter through Antonia's insides. Warning signals went off all through her. *This wasn't just a Saturday morning ride, and Daniel wasn't just one of her clients. It was a date, and he made her feel like a teenager when he smiled at her.*

Antonia knew she was getting into dangerous territory and ought to pull away right now. *The feelings she had around him were much too intense for com-*

fort—or security. Yet she could not seem to make herself take that step back. She could not quell the excitement and anticipation rising within her.

They approached the bottom of the mesa, where a line of greenery indicated the presence of water. As they neared the mesa, however, Antonia could see that whatever water there might be was nowhere visible. There was a shallow creek bed, along the edge of which were stretched a few larger mesquite bushes and even a tall cottonwood tree, but the bed was dry and cracked.

"Wet weather creek," Daniel explained. "This time of year, it should have some water in it, but..." He shrugged, his voice trailing away.

Antonia did not need an explanation. She was well aware of the drought that had been plaguing Texas for quite some time now. It was the bane of her clients' existence; local ranchers were having to sell off cattle they could not afford to feed because the lack of rain had killed off not only much of the natural vegetation their cattle fed upon but also the hay they raised to supplement their feed. Purchasing feed for the animals quickly wiped out all profit. In a vicious cycle, selling off the cattle drove the prices even lower, with the result that more than one local rancher had been driven out of the business entirely.

"At least it's still shady," Daniel commented. "You want to get down and rest a spell? There's a nice spot to sit over on that rock."

He nodded toward a large rock with a flat top at the edge of the dry creek that was shaded by the cottonwood tree. They dismounted and tied their horses' reins to a nearby mesquite bush, then crossed the dry creek to sit on the rock. A breeze stirred the air, lifting Antonia's hair and cooling her cheek. It was a soft, pleasant spring day, with everything turning green around them. The mesa rose behind them in an almost sheer cliff, and on all three other sides, the land stretched away to the horizon, flat and tan, dotted with green bushes and an occasional stand of trees. The sky was bright blue, with little white wisps of clouds. It was peaceful and expansive.

Antonia crooked her knee, setting her heel against the rock, and circled her upraised knee with her arms, contemplating the scenery around her. Beside her, Daniel braced his hand against the rock, leaning back.

"It's beautiful out here," Antonia commented softly.

"Mmm-hmm. Beautiful."

Antonia turned her head to look at Daniel and saw that he was watching her as he spoke, the underlying meaning of his words clear in his eyes. It was a little thing, and Antonia had been told more than once before that she was beautiful, but somehow the word from this taciturn rancher made her heart leap in response. She could feel the heat rushing into her cheeks, and she cursed her fair skin that showed everything she felt.

"I meant the land," she said with as much severity as she could muster.

"It's beautiful, too," Daniel replied. His eyes drifted down over her face. "But I'd rather look at you."

Antonia gazed back at him, unable to pull away. He

leaned forward, and she knew that he was going to kiss her. Something deep inside told her it was a bad idea, that this was her last chance to back out. But even as a warning voice whined that she would regret it, she knew that she would not stop him. She wanted Daniel to kiss her. She wanted to kiss him back. She was, at that moment, alive in an exciting and electric way that she had not felt in years.

His lips touched hers and clung. It was a soft, almost tentative kiss, without the force of pent-up emotion that had permeated their first kiss the other day. His mouth was gentle, exploratory, easing gradually into heat and hunger. She relaxed into him, kissing him back, feeling the fever between them grow. His hands cupped her face, then sank into her hair, holding her still as his mouth grew more and more eager. They kissed again and again, tongues clashing and caressing, their breath coming shorter in their throats. He pulled her to him, burying his lips in hers, a low moan escaping him.

Heat exploded through Antonia, rushing throughout her body. She shook under the force of her fierce hunger, all the nerve endings in her skin suddenly tinglingly alive. She threw her arms around Daniel's neck, pressing her body up into his, loving the feel of his hard, muscular body against her softer one, aching to feel more. His hands moved down, caressing her body through her clothes, gliding over her back and hips and legs, then moving back up her sides until settling on her breasts.

He cupped her breasts, squeezing the fleshy mounds gently, and Antonia's nipples tightened in response.

Her breasts were full and aching beneath his touch, her nipples hardening with desire.

"Antonia..." He breathed her name as his lips left hers and began to travel downward, trailing over the soft white flesh of her throat.

Antonia shivered at the touch of his lips, letting her head fall back to expose the full length of her throat to him. His arm went around her back, supporting her, as his other hand went under her shirt and up to caress her breasts. Only the lace of her bra separated her skin from his, and the contrast of the faint roughness of the lace against the supremely soft flesh of her breasts excited him. His breath shuddered out harshly.

Daniel quickly unbuttoned her shirt and kissed his way across her skin, exploring the texture and taste of her, velvet soft over the hard bones of her rib cage. He reached at last the upswelling of her breast, pillowy soft. He nuzzled beneath the lacy edge of her top, drunk with the scent and feel of her. Antonia twined her fingers through his hair, clenching them as a new frisson of pleasure darted through her.

She felt giddy and wild, teetering on the edge of a precipice. She wanted to make the leap, to let go and fall into the heat and passion of the moment. Yet even as she relaxed, giving in to the moment, some other part of her jerked back, scared of the dizzying sensation of freefall. Antonia tightened, and her mind began to work again. *Whatever was she doing out here in the middle of nowhere, necking like a teenager with Daniel Sutton? It was ridiculous, impossible. It didn't matter how good it felt—where could it lead? Did she intend to have wild sex right here on this rock? On their first date?*

''No,'' she murmured, her hands coming down and bracing against his chest. ''Wait.''

Daniel froze, his breath rasping in his throat. Slowly he raised his head and looked into her eyes. His dark brown gaze burned with a fierce flame.

''We can't,'' she said a little desperately, aware suddenly of the iron strength of his arm, the firm wall of his chest beneath her hands. Daniel Sutton was a strong man, and at this moment there was a wildness in his eyes that nudged awake her deepest fears.

He relaxed, letting out a muffled curse, and his arms fell away from her. He moved back.

''I'm sorry.''

''No. Wait—I didn't mean—'' Antonia pushed back her hair, feeling suddenly bereft, as if she had lost something important. ''I'm sorry. It's just—this time, this place.'' She glanced around at the empty landscape. ''It's too early. For me, I mean.... Oh, you must think I'm hopelessly muddled.''

Daniel chuckled, surprising her. ''Actually, I kind of like you muddled. Makes you human, like the rest of us.''

''Makes me human?'' Antonia looked at him, startled. ''What am I the rest of the time?''

''Oh, you know, above us lesser mortals. Beautiful, intelligent, cool, calm.''

''Is that what I seem like? A snob?''

''No, not a snob. Just...sort of perfect. The kind of person who doesn't make mistakes.''

Antonia let out a wry laugh. "Believe me, I have made tons of mistakes. Horrible ones."

"Somehow I doubt that."

"It's true."

"What? Tell me some big, horrible mistake you made."

"Well, my ex-husband, for one," Antonia retorted.

"Ah. So you have one of those, too."

"I told you, I'm anything but perfect." She slid off the rock, straightening her clothes. "That's just...a mask, I guess, that poised, aloof thing. Part of it was the way I was raised—'a lady doesn't cry,' 'a lady doesn't scream and hop about'—and part of it was being a woman in vet school. I couldn't let things faze me or everyone would think it proved I didn't have the right stuff to be a veterinarian. I'm sorry. I don't mean to come off stiff...."

"You don't," Daniel assured her, sliding off the rock to stand beside her. He put his hands on her shoulders and turned her to face him. "I wasn't criticizing you. I like it when you look like a princess." He smiled down at her. "It's a challenge, you know? Makes me think about melting that reserve." The fierce light was there again in his eyes, then gone as he went on. "But I like it when you're muddled, too. We can go slow. Folks will tell you that I'm none too fast-moving anyway. We can do whatever you like."

He slid his arms around her loosely, cuddling her, his cheek resting against her hair. It was awfully nice, Antonia thought, to be with a man tall enough to do that. It was, in fact, awfully nice in every way to be with Daniel Sutton. There was no reason to be on edge or to pull back. She leaned her head against his chest.

"I like this," she admitted.

"We could go on doing this a while, then."

"Okay." Antonia smiled and slid her arms around his waist. *This was a very good place to be.*

Chapter 5

They rode back to the house, and Daniel threw together sandwiches for lunch. Two of James's friends were there, and she could hear the reverberation of a heavy bass all the way from his room.

"And his door's closed, believe it or not," Daniel told her wryly, casting a pained look toward in the general direction of his son's room. "I'll go tell him to turn it down."

"That's okay. I don't mind." In fact, the steady vibration was a little annoying, but Antonia wasn't about to say anything that would cause friction between Daniel and his son, and she figured that after a few minutes the vibration would probably become part of the background, like a clock ticking.

"Really?" Daniel turned to look at her. She nodded, and he returned to his sandwich making, saying,

"I can't stand it. Just sounds like this 'boom, boom, boom' all the time. No music."

He turned, plates in hand, and crossed to the table, grinning. "I sound like my father now. Parenthood does terrible things to you."

He put the plates on the table and went back to the refrigerator for drinks. "You know..." he began in a supremely casual voice, glancing quickly at her as he set down the drinks, then away. "I was thinking...if you really can stand that noise..."

"Yes?" Antonia asked, intrigued by his manner.

He glanced at her again, then said quickly, "I was thinking maybe you'd be willing to, uh, go with me to a dance. Sort of."

"Sort of?" Antonia's brows went up. "Sort of go with you? Or sort of a dance?"

"I'm not sure," he admitted. "I'm really bad at this. It's, well, you probably won't like it, and I wouldn't expect you to want to go. So feel free to refuse."

"You're making this sound delightful so far."

"What it is, is...I'm asking you to the senior prom."

"Excuse me?"

He smiled, giving a little shrug. "I have to chaperone the senior prom next weekend. I was on the committee, and that was one of the few things I thought I could do. Decorations were clearly out of my league. So I have to go, and it would be really nice to have some company—I mean, somebody I could talk to. And since you said you could stand the music, I thought, well, maybe you wouldn't mind." He looked at her again.

"Well...let me think." Antonia propped her elbows on the table and set her chin on her hand in a contemplative attitude. "Would I get a corsage out of this?"

"Absolutely." He smiled, his eyes starting to twinkle.

"And do I get to wear a long dress?"

"Of course."

"And do I get to dance?"

"If you have the courage."

"I have to admit—it sounds pretty good. At least I wouldn't be taller than my partner, like I always was in high school."

"True. Being taller than my date has always been one of my major selling points."

"Okay," Antonia said and grinned. "I'll go to the senior prom with you."

He grinned back. "Great. I'll be the envy of every guy there."

Antonia picked up her sandwich and bit into it. "Mmm. This is good."

"I'm a hand at making sandwiches. My other specialty is frozen dinners."

"I'm pretty good at those, too. You don't cook?"

"Well, yeah, I do. You're kind of forced to with a kid. Not anything fancy, though—mostly chili, spaghetti, stew, sloppy joes, anything that can be done in one of those slow cookers. One-dish meals. There used to be this lady, Señora Alvarez, who'd come every couple of weeks and make us a bunch of dinners and freeze them, and those would get me through about half our meals. They were good, too—carne guisada, enchiladas verde, tamales. But then she went to live with her daughter in Houston. Man, I was sorry to see her go.''

They talked and laughed through lunch. Just as they finished and were cleaning up, James and his friends came clattering down the stairs and into the kitchen. James introduced Antonia to the other two boys, Dolan and Benny, who turned out to be the nephew Rita had spoken of. The boys were in need of refueling, which appeared to be a massive effort involving not only sandwiches and chips, but also a leftover casserole and half a pie.

Daniel saw Antonia's amazed survey of the food piled onto the table, and he laughed. ''Teenage boys. The main thing about cooking for them, I've found, is fix a lot.''

After the three young men pounded back up the stairs with their loot, Antonia said, ''Well, I'd better go now.''

She realized that she was rather reluctant to leave, but she couldn't think of any reason to delay her departure. She had already stayed longer than an invitation to ride probably meant.

''Oh. Well. Thank you for coming out here.''

''Thank you for inviting me,'' Antonia replied, wishing she didn't sound so stiff and awkward. The problem was, she didn't know what to do when she left. An hour or two ago, they had been kissing madly, yet here they were back under the same roof as Daniel's son and his friends.

Obviously Daniel suffered from the same malady.

He followed her out to her SUV, opening her door for her and then standing with the door open, making awkward conversation.

"So I'll pick you up next Friday for the prom?" he asked. "I have to be there before the kids arrive."

"Sure." Antonia looked at him, then glanced up at the second story of the house.

Daniel grinned at her gesture. "James's room is on the other side. They can't see us."

He leaned in and kissed her, his mouth warm and full of promise. Then he pulled back, winked at her, and closed the door.

Antonia started the car and drove off, unable to suppress her smile.

It was no surprise to Daniel that a few hours after Antonia left his house, his brother Quinn turned up on his doorstep. He was surprised only that Quinn had not visited him the other evening after Daniel had had lunch with Antonia.

Quinn held up the six pack of beer bottles he carried, grinning. "Peace offering?"

"What for?" Daniel asked, stepping back so that he could enter the kitchen. "I'm not mad at you…yet."

"Yeah. But I figure you probably will be before the evening's through, so I might as well come prepared."

Daniel had to smile. It was hard to withstand his brother's charm. Quinn had always been one who could talk himself out of almost any situation, a quality Daniel admired while at the same time regarding with some suspicion.

Quinn, the third oldest of the Sutton brothers, was a handsome man, slightly shorter than Daniel, with dark red hair and a temper to match. His good nature and his wit, fortunately, were as quick to return as his temper. He had been the one most likely to get into trouble when they were younger, and Daniel had more than once had to rescue Quinn when his charm had not been enough to get him out. It had been something of a surprise to them all, therefore, when Quinn had decided to go into law enforcement. He had been on the police force in San Antonio for several years and had been advancing quickly, but he could not stand life in the city and had returned a few years earlier to Angel Eye, run for sheriff and won.

"You're probably right," Daniel responded. "You usually do end up irritating me some way."

Quinn just grinned, unperturbed, and handed his brother a beer. He took another one for himself and put the remainder in the refrigerator. Daniel led the way into the den, and they sat down.

Daniel felt relatively sure that Quinn was there on an information-gathering mission about Antonia Campbell, but he decided perversely not to help him get into the subject. Instead he just leaned back in his chair and took a swig of his beer, looking at Quinn.

"Where's that rascally nephew of mine?" Quinn asked.

"Upstairs studying—I hope. All I know he's doing for sure is damaging his eardrums with that music of his. Do you get this hip-hop thing?"

Quinn laughed. "You're talking to the wrong boy there, big brother. All I know about kids' music is that they play it way too loud in the grocery store parking lot at night, and we have to go over and tell them to pipe down.''

''It seems like he could at least listen to country,'' Daniel grumbled.

''Careful. You're turning into an old man. You know, the kind who told you *Kiss* was the tool of the devil.''

Daniel's mouth quirked up at the memory. ''Yeah. Mr. Satterfield, down at the drugstore. Was he a ever a sour old coot! Okay, I'll stop griping about James's music.''

They were quiet for a long moment. Quinn regarded his older brother over the top of his beer bottle, then finally said, ''So...the vet, huh?''

''Excuse me?''

''Don't try that impassive trick with me. You know what I'm asking—what's going on with you and the oh-so-attractive Dr. Campbell? Everyone in town's got you in the sack with her. They're all asking me, and it's pretty embarrassing that I didn't even know you'd been dating her. Lena had to fill me in on all the gossip.''

''As if Lena knows.''

''Are you kidding? Lena knows everything there is to know. She probably knows more about your affair than you do.''

''Hardly an affair.''

''Ah-ah! So that means you haven't—''

''Good Lord, Quinn! The woman came out here today to ride horses. That's all.''

‘‘All? When was the last time you invited a woman out here to ride?’’

‘‘I don’t know. But it’s happened before. It doesn’t mean anything. I happened to run into her one day at the Moonstone and sat down at the booth with her.’’

‘‘Mmm. ’Cause it was so crowded, no doubt.’’ Quinn’s mahogany-colored eyes danced.

Daniel crossed his arms and looked at his brother with raised brows. ‘‘Yeah. So what?’’

‘‘So what a crock,’’ Quinn retorted without heat. ‘‘If you think that I would believe you drove into town to eat at the Moonstone Café and just happened to arrive at the same time as Dr. Campbell and just happened to sit with her because it was so crowded, then you’re crazy. Or stupid. I’m not sure which.’’

‘‘I was already in town,’’ Daniel said defensively.

‘‘So you saw her truck at the café and you decided to stop and see her, maybe wangle an invitation to eat with her. Right?’’

‘‘I’m not telling you anything.’’

‘‘I’m not going to tell anybody, for Pete’s sake. I just want to know that I know the real story when they ask me.’’

‘‘Forget it.’’

‘‘I’m your brother!’’ Quinn assumed an offended air.

‘‘Yeah, and your dispatcher is Lena Daniels.’’ Daniel snorted. ‘‘She would have the information out of you in two seconds.’’

‘‘You certainly don’t show much faith in your own brother,’’ Quinn commented, looking pained. ‘‘I *am* a trained professional, you know. I'm chock full of secrets."

"Right. Things so boring Lena isn't interested."

"How did you get to be such a hard man, Daniel? The rest of our family is nice."

"Having you for a younger brother made me that way," Daniel retorted.

Quinn just waited, watching him, swigging his beer. Finally Daniel groaned. "Oh, hell, Quinn...."

Quinn grinned and sat up straighter. "So? How serious is it?"

"Not serious. I told you, we haven't really dated."

"What was that thing with her coming out here to ride?"

"That's not a date. She likes to ride, and she lives in town, so she can't keep a horse. So I asked if she'd like to come out here to ride. That's all."

"When are you having a real date?"

Daniel smiled faintly. "Next week. We're going to help chaperone the prom."

"You're dragging her along to chaperone James's prom?" Quinn asked scornfully.

"She wanted to go," Daniel retorted.

Quinn shook his head, but said, "Well, I guess for you that represents progress." He paused, then said, "She's a knockout."

"Mmm-hmm."

"Got that Grace Kelly thing going."

"Yeah."

"Kind of different from Lurleen."

"True."

"Getting stuff out of you is like digging for gold,"

Quinn said disgustedly. "I've had crooks confess easier than you'll talk about your love life."

"That's because I have no love life."

Quinn cocked an eyebrow.

"Okay," Daniel admitted. "Maybe I have the possibility of a love life."

"You want to know what I think?"

"Probably not."

Quinn pointed at him with the top of his bottle. "You're hooked on this one. I can tell."

"Yeah? How's that?"

"You're not much of a talker, true, but you're not usually this close-mouthed, not with me. There's something special about this lady. You're afraid to start talking for fear of what you'll say."

Daniel cursed, feeling a flush rising in his cheeks. Quinn let out a crow of triumph. "I knew it!"

"You don't know anything," Daniel retorted. He paused, then said quietly, "I haven't felt like this in a long time, Quinn. I thought I was too old."

Quinn snorted. "I don't think you can get too old to feel like that."

"When I saw her, it was like somebody hit me with a ton of bricks. You know?"

"Yeah, I know."

Daniel cast him a sideways glance. "You would. You're always hot for some girl. You're as bad as James."

"Hey! Give me a break. I don't fall in love every other week. At least, not since I was twenty or so."

Daniel grinned. "Maybe not. But you have to admit

there's hardly a woman in Angel Eye or Hammond under the age of forty whom you haven't romanced."

"Now that's a lie. 'Sides, can I help it if women fall for my boyish charm and good looks? Anyway, we're talking about you, not me. And the enchanting lady vet. When do I get to meet Dr. Campbell? Or am I going to have to take Jo-Jo in for some imaginary illness?"

Daniel looked pained. "Don't do that. I'd be embarrassed to see her again if she found out my brother has a cat for a pet. Come on, man, you're the sheriff. You should have a German shepherd or something. At least a Lab."

"Jo-Jo could whip any Lab's butt," Quinn retorted good-naturedly, long used to his brothers' friendly teasing.

Daniel, who had more than once felt Jo-Jo's claws sink into his leg, grinned and admitted, "That's true. Solo won't even get out of the truck at your house." Despite his size, the mutt, acquired from the pound when James was eight and enthusiastically named after a *Star Wars* character, was a coward at heart.

Quinn grinned. "I know. I've seen him. Jo-Jo knows she's got him psyched out. Every time she sees him out there, her tail starts twitching. She's pretty disappointed not to get a chance to chase him around the house. But you keep trying to sidetrack me. The question is, when do I get to meet her?" Quinn prodded. "'Course, I guess I could stop her sometime to check her license and registration."

"Cool your jets. You'll meet her. Once I'm sure it won't scare her away."

"Very funny." Quinn set his empty beer bottle on the end table beside him. He looked at his brother, the laughter gone from his face. "This sounds sort of serious."

Daniel began to pick at the label on his bottle, looking at it as if he was absorbed in the action. Finally he said. "I don't know about serious. I doubt I'll ever be serious about a woman again."

"Why the hell not? Lurleen's been gone for years."

"It's not that. It's just...I'm too old to jump into something, even if she did give me a jolt."

"Don't have to jump," Quinn pointed out reasonably. "You can proceed at your usual snail's pace if you want to."

"She's not interested in moving fast, either."

"How do you know that?"

Daniel shrugged. "I don't know. She blows hot and cold."

"So? She's a woman. You probably don't remember what they're like, it having been so long since you spent any time with one."

"Shut up," Daniel replied without heat. "I'm serious. This morning she seemed real—well, like she was pretty interested—"

"Okay...."

"But then she got all stiff and pulled away."

"You ask why?"

Daniel shook his head.

"I've always found that that's a good way to learn things."

"I don't want to push her. She's...different. She's not like any other woman I've ever met."

"Don't meet too many women vets," Quinn agreed.

"It's not just that. I've been around other career women. Our sister isn't exactly the clinging, dependent type, you know."

"You're telling me." Quinn had had more than his share of arguments with his sister, who shared both his red hair and his ready emotions.

"She doesn't intimidate me." He paused, then added honestly, "Not exactly. It's just...you know, she always looks like she just stepped out of a magazine—hair perfect, slacks creased. But it's not just that, either, 'cause I've seen her all covered with blood and—"

"I get the picture."

"But she still has that cool, aloof air. She was a debutante, you know."

"Really? An actual one?"

Daniel nodded. "Her family's wealthy and East Coast. Her mother spends her life doing charity stuff. She's got class, any way you look at it. And here I am, just an old horse wrangler from Texas."

"Well, that gives you some advantage," Quinn said with a grin. "Being from Texas, I mean."

Daniel grimaced, and Quinn added seriously, "Look, so you didn't go to charity balls all your life. I wouldn't think she's all that big on that life. If she was, she wouldn't be a vet or living in Angel Eye. Right? I mean, you two can sit around and talk about fetlocks and bloodlines and colic, all that kind of stuff."

Daniel chuckled. "I'm sure that will win her heart."

"All I'm saying is—she is the woman she is now,

not some eighteen-year-old wearing a white ball gown and doing…whatever it is debutantes do.''

''I know. But I'm not real good with women, anyway—you know that. And somebody like her…''

''So what're you saying? You going to give up on her? Does that mean she's free, 'cause, like I said, she's one fine-looking—''

''Don't even think about it.'' Daniel fixed his brother with a look that would have dropped most men in their tracks.

Quinn just gazed at him, his eyes dancing with devilish amusement. ''What? I thought you weren't—''

''You know good and well I'm not going to stop seeing her. I'm just saying don't expect anything serious to come of this.''

''I'll reserve judgment on that,'' Quinn responded. He rose, picking up the empty beer bottle. ''All right. I guess I've pumped you for all the information I can. I better head on home. I promised Mrs. Mendoza I'd make a pass down her street as I drove home. She's decided they're dealing drugs down the block from her.''

''Are they?''

Quinn shrugged. ''I guess they could be. But she calls the office about three times a week on the average. Burglars, drug dealers, Peeping Toms, you name it. I think she just likes to have somebody come out and talk to her. She's lonely since her husband died last year. Her daughter only comes down from Dallas about once a year.''

''Ah, the life of a sheriff in Burton County.''

''I know. It's full of danger and excitement.''

Quinn walked into the kitchen, Daniel following him. Quinn tossed the empty bottle in the trash and opened the back door, then turned, pointing a warning finger at his brother. "Now, remember, I better get to meet this lady soon—or she's going to meet my cat."

"You've got me quaking in my boots."

Quinn clattered down the steps and out to his patrol car. Daniel smiled to himself. He could always count on Quinn to keep him amused. There were times when Daniel marveled that any brother of his could be so glib.

Daniel turned to the sink and began to rinse off the plates from supper and put them away in the dishwasher. He had just finished and closed the dishwasher when there was a knock on the kitchen door. Thinking it was Quinn who had turned around and come back for some reason, he opened the door.

The flippant greeting that had been forming in his mouth died. It was his father who stood on the kitchen stoop. "Dad!"

He stepped back, holding the door open. "Come on in."

His father, an older, grayer version of himself in jeans and a plaid shirt, cowboy hat on his head, stepped inside. He took off the hat. "Daniel."

"Want a beer?" Daniel asked. "Quinn brought some over and left them."

Marshall Sutton shook his head and glanced around the kitchen. After a moment he sat down at the table. Daniel sat down across from him. He wasn't sure why his father was here. He wasn't much of one for visiting—and even less for idle chitchat.

"Well..." Daniel began when his father said nothing. "How you doing?"

"Fine," Marshall responded laconically. "You?"

"I'm good."

There was a moment of silence, then Marshall said, "Heard you been seeing the vet."

"Oh," Daniel said, the light dawning. "You know, you probably should have just come with Quinn. That way I would only have had to say it once."

"Say what? Quinn was here today?"

"Yeah. He was asking about Antonia, too."

"Yeah?" A half smile quirked his father's mouth. "Bet he spent a mite more time jawing about it."

Daniel grinned. "Yeah."

"She came out to the ranch a couple of weeks ago," Marshall Sutton volunteered. "Good-looking woman."

"Yeah, she is."

"You like her?" His father turned his piercing dark gaze on Daniel.

"Yes."

Marshall nodded thoughtfully. "Well...that's good."

"Yeah."

"All right, then." Marshall stood up and clapped his hand on his son's shoulder. "Better be getting back home. It's about my bedtime."

"Okay. Glad you dropped by."

"Sure." Marshall walked to the door and turned. "Bring her by the house sometime."

"Okay."

With a nod, the older man left. Daniel shook his head, smiling, and took one of Quinn's beers out of the fridge. *All that was missing was a call from Cater and Cory. And Beth.*

That would come, too, he assured himself as he strolled back into the den—as soon as one of them talked to Quinn. But for all his protestations, Daniel knew that he didn't really mind. His family's concern was warming. Besides, he realized that he rather liked everyone knowing he was dating Antonia Campbell. He felt, well, a little proud, he supposed.

Daniel smiled to himself, taking a swig of beer. *Talk about feeling like a teenager again.* He realized that he was sitting there, grinning at the wall like an idiot, but the fact only made him grin harder. He hadn't felt this good in years. *And he intended to make damn sure he continued feeling that way.*

Antonia lay on the couch, Mitzi curled up beside her, and lazily flipped through the channels on the television. Nothing held her attention long; she was, she knew, too distracted to even concentrate on a television show. She wasn't sure what she felt or what she wanted, a curious state for her. Antonia prided herself on the calm, even mundane pace of her life. She had had enough excitement to last her a lifetime during her marriage. Peace and stability were her watchwords. Yet here she was, thoughts skittering every which way, confused and distracted. And, even stranger, she was not upset or irritated by her state. *She felt, well, excited and happy more than anything else.*

She had driven home from Daniel Sutton's house this afternoon in a curious state of delight and trepidation. She was excited, scared, eager, foolish, hesitant—all at the same time. She had taken a long, soaking bath, hoping it would bring some clarity to her mind. Instead, she had found herself lazily lying in the bathtub for the better part of an hour, daydreaming about Daniel Sutton and smiling.

She had tried to scold herself back into her usual practical mode, but it hadn't worked. She had spent the remainder of the day lackadaisically going through her weekend chores, a muted hum of excitement running through her. After she fed the cat, she had settled down to read, but she had been unable to concentrate. So she had finally turned on the television, only to find that it could not penetrate her pleasantly befogged mind, either.

She clicked off the remote and lay for a while simply staring at the blank screen. *What was she going to do?* It seemed bizarre to her that she didn't know the answer. She was the sort who went straight for the solution and then did whatever was necessary. She was not a ditherer.

Or, at least, she hadn't been since she left Alan.

The thought was enough to send a chill through her. Antonia straightened up, crossing her arms. That was the whole crux of the problem, really—she had sworn never to be foolish about a man again. She would not let herself get swept away by a nice smile or a certain amount of charm. She would never fall into that trap of giving herself heart and soul to a man, letting him become the be-all and end-all of her universe. Never again would she let her heart make her vulnerable.

For four years it had not been a problem to stick to her plans. She had dated but kept herself heart-whole. She had never felt the least danger to her autonomy or her contentment. She had been in complete control of her life, and no man had been more than a fairly enjoyable sideshow. But in only a few days, Daniel Sutton had shaken up her life.

When he had kissed her the other day, she had been stunned by the passion she had felt. However, she had mentally written if off as a fluke. It had been the time and place, she had told herself, the elation of having saved the mare and foal, that had made the sensations that sizzled through her seem so earth-shaking. Today, however, she could not dismiss it so easily. There had been no such extenuating circumstances. Yet she had trembled with the force of her desire. She had wanted to fling caution to the winds and make love with Daniel right there and then. Reason and temperance had not played the slightest part in her decision. Indeed, she had not really made any decision. She had been ruled by hunger, then fear had stopped her—fear of the force of her own emotions. Her head had scarcely been involved at all. *And when Daniel had smiled and told her that they would take things as slowly as she wanted, she had practically melted into a puddle of schoolgirl goo.*

Antonia tried to work up some righteous indignation at the memory, but she found herself smiling instead. Daniel had asked her out again, and she had agreed—again without any thought.

She knew that she should be weighing her decision—making a sensible list of the pros and cons of dating Daniel Sutton and coming to a thoughtful conclusion, not sitting around thinking of how he had looked and what he had said and getting all fluttery over it. Yet she couldn't even get upset at her own lack of organization and control. She was, quite simply, enjoying the feelings of the moment and not at all inclined to be analytical.

She would think about it some other time, she told herself. Sometime when she was feeling more rational and less—well, less *fizzy.*

The phone rang, startling Antonia. She reached for it with equal parts excitement at the thought that it might be Daniel calling her and dread that it was more likely the clinic with some emergency.

"Hello?"

There was an empty silence on the other end.

"Hello?"

Again there was no reply. Antonia waited, gripping the receiver tightly. It sounded as if the line was open; there wasn't the blank, dead quality of a call that had not gone through. She almost thought she could hear someone breathing.

"Hello? Is someone there?"

Antonia slammed the receiver down. Her heart raced, all contentment fled. *It wasn't possible. It wasn't possible.* But all she could think was, *Alan's found me.*

Chapter 6

Antonia was in high spirits the following Friday as she got ready to go to the dance. It had made her giggle a little inside to think that she was going to a prom with Daniel. She might be eleven years out of high school, but even so, she could feel some of the humming excitement that the young girls must feel. It had been building all week, and even the two silent phone calls she had received had not been able to kick her completely out of her happy state. *So what if she was a chaperone, not a student?* She still got to dress up, after all, in a lovely soft thirties-style gown of the type Jean Harlow had worn. Sleek and silvery, it had a deeply scooped out back, held together by two thin crisscrossed straps, and a fish-tail hem in the back. Her long hair was up in a soft French roll, anchored on the side by a long, stylized rhinestone clip. She looked, she thought with a pleased smile, very romantic and feminine, something she rarely had an opportunity to do. She would get to dance a little, if she was lucky. But best of all, she would be able to spend the evening in Daniel's company.

That was something she had been thinking about all week. She had been thinking far too much about it, truth to tell. She would have been embarrassed for anyone to know how often images of Daniel had crept into her mind, even when she should have been concentrating on her work. She remembered his kisses, the way his eyes twinkled when he smiled, the way his callused hand felt sliding over her bare arm. More than once, sitting at her desk, working on papers, she found herself drifting off into a dream world. She was, she supposed, as bad as any high school senior, unable to concentrate on her studies for thinking about the prom.

Daniel came to pick her up early Friday evening. She opened the door to find him looking handsome in a tux, a small box in one hand. Antonia smiled, and her grin grew broader at the involuntary widening of Daniel's eyes and his quick indrawn breath when he saw her. The dress had made exactly the statement she had hoped for.

"You're beautiful. It isn't fair. You'll put all those poor high school girls in the shade at their own prom."

"I doubt that." But Antonia could not help but be warmed by his praise. The look on his face had told her that his words were exactly how he felt. "Come in."

Daniel walked inside, glancing around at the small living room with its old-fashioned wood plank floors, polished to a golden gleam. ''I like your house.'' He nodded back toward the front porch. ''Nice shady porch. You sit out there a lot in the evenings?''

Antonia nodded. ''Yeah. It's peaceful. There's a honeysuckle bush at one end, and it smells divine. I've been thinking about getting a porch swing.''

He glanced down, a little surprised, as Mitzi came up and began to twine herself around his legs. ''Why, hello, kitty.''

''It's terrible how shy she is around strangers,'' Antonia said wryly. ''Careful, she'll get hair all over your tux.''

''That's okay. I can brush it off.''

Daniel handed her the small box he carried, and when Antonia opened it, she saw that it was a corsage of fuchsia-throated white orchids, fragile and lovely. He fastened it to her wrist, their heads so close they almost touched. She could smell the scent of his cologne, feel the heat of his hands, and she was amazed all over again at the effect he had on her.

He raised his head, and their eyes met. He smiled and kissed her once, hard and quick. ''Come on, we better go or I'll forget what I'm supposed to be doing.''

They went to dinner first, at a steak house in Hammond, then drove to the high school gymnasium. As the first shift of chaperones, they, along with two sets of parents, three teachers and the principal, had to arrive before the students.

Inside, the gym was strung with crepe paper, and scattered around the floor were cardboard cutouts of palm trees and Egyptian pyramids. Not one but *three* mirror balls revolved slowly over the dance floor, which was lighted in a muted way by red and blue spotlights. A raised platform at one end held a DJ and his mix machine, hired out of San Antonio. He was still setting up and nodded a harried hello at them when they walked in. At the opposite end of the gym, where the lighting was unromantically bright, were a buffet table and white trellis, where a photographer was setting up to take pictures of happy couples.

The students began to trickle in, and before long the room was filled with girls in prom dresses and upswept hairdos and boys in tuxes—often accompanied with cowboy boots—dancing to heavy-bassed hip-hop tunes, interspersed with disco tunes, eighties hits and country songs. The theme, Antonia decided, was some sort of "The Nile Meets Modern South Texas." Everyone seemed to be having a good time, however, including her.

Daniel's role was to loiter by one of the exits to prevent kids from slipping out to the parking lot to indulge in alcoholic beverages, then reentering the dance. The other dads and an English teacher, who looked as if she had taught at the school since World War II and had never once cracked a smile, manned the other exits, while the moms took tickets, and the other teachers and the principal roamed the floor.

It was somewhat excessive security, Antonia thought, for the students seemed a largely peaceable lot. Daniel had to tell only one young man that he could not go out the exit door, and as the evening wore on with no more incidents, he and Antonia slipped out onto the dance floor once or twice when a slow number came on. Those moments were sweet, and she didn't even mind when one of the kids dancing by whistled under his breath as if he were shocked by the sight of grownups slow-dancing under the spangled light.

The music was too loud and the punch too sweet, and Antonia supposed she should have been bored. But, in fact, she was having a wonderful time. It was intriguing—and faintly surreal—to watch the teenagers as they danced and talked and laughed. They were only twelve or thirteen years younger than she—and a whole lifetime away. She felt an oddly maternal pride, watching Daniel's son, easily the handsomest boy in the room. He and several of the other boys asked her to dance, and she did so, feeling faintly foolish but enjoying it, too. Around midnight, Mr. Cox, the algebra teacher, cut loose in a passable merengue with one of the senior girls, which set everyone in the room to clapping furiously and made Antonia wonder if perhaps the teachers should have been checked for slipping off to their cars for a nip or two.

In another attempt to combat drinking, the dance continued until four o'clock in the morning, at which time the Moonstone Café would be open for a senior breakfast. Daniel's chaperonage shift was over at midnight, with another set moving in for the middle-of-the-night watch. After the impromptu merengue, Daniel and Antonia left. Outside the building, the hush of the night was a startling contrast to the raucous noise inside. The sky was clear, the stars winking brightly in its darkness. The sky in Angel Eye was vast, Antonia had discovered, and the stars as bright and noticeable as the Spanish explorers had indicated when they named the area.

Daniel left the parking lot of the high school and turned left, taking the highway that led out of town. "Thought we might go out to my place."

Antonia glanced over at him. "Your place, huh? Is this the big seduction scene?"

His grin was white in the darkness, and he cast a look over at her. "Maybe a little one. Mostly there's just something I wanted to show you. And when you get right down to it, it's on my dad's place, actually."

Antonia was intrigued. "What is it?"

"You'll see." He chuckled at her curious expression. "Seems I've found out how to get your attention."

Antonia made a face at him and settled back in her seat. Whatever Daniel had planned, she felt sure it was nothing she needed to worry about. There was something vaguely exciting about hurtling through the dark emptiness toward an unknown destination, and she decided that she would simply enjoy it. She had been thinking all week about being with Daniel again—hearing his voice, seeing his face, sensations heightened as they always were with him, so that she seemed to constantly feel a low hum of anticipation all through her.

After a while he turned off the road and rattled across a cattle guard. After that their progress was much slower as they made their way along the drive that led to Marshall Sutton's house. They veered off onto another track as they neared the house. It grew more and more indistinguishable as any sort of path, until finally they were simply driving across the land. He slowed down even more to ease the jars and bumps. Looking out the window, Antonia could see the dark shapes of cows here and there, usually clustered together. They passed a stock tank with a windmill, and before long the truck was climbing up a low rise.

About three-fourths of the way up, Daniel stopped. ''We'll have to walk from here.''

Antonia cast an expressive look down at her evening gown and sandals. ''Like this?''

''Yeah, sure, it's an easy walk. The ground is a big slab of rock, really, no dirt and vegetation.'' He smiled. ''If it gets too bad, I'll carry you. How's that?''

''That's a deal.'' Antonia slid out of the cab of the truck. Daniel reached into the bed of the pickup and pulled out a blanket, then opened a cooler and removed a bottle of champagne, along with two glasses.

''My, my,'' Antonia commented. ''I think we *are* talking seduction here.''

''You've got a one-track mind, Doc. We're talking celebration. Getting through the prom. And a little present for you for giving up your evening.''

''I didn't have anything exciting planned.''

He led her up the incline of rocky ground to the top. It was, as he had said, rather easy. When they reached the edge of the rocky bluff, she saw that on the other side the land fell away steeply, so that they had a commanding view of a large stretch of land before them. The scene was washed in moonlight, giving it an eerie beauty.

Daniel popped the cork of the champagne and poured the fizzing drink into the glasses, handing her one.

"To the end of high school," he said, smiling and raising his glass. "There were times, I'll tell you, when I never thought I would see the day. It was better this time around, I think. I had company."

Antonia smiled, raising her glass to his. She took a sip of the cold liquid, feeling the bubbles slide enticingly over her tongue, and looked out at the view. It was as if they were alone in the universe, surrounded by the vast emptiness of the sky and the land. Daniel spread out the blanket, and she sat down, shivering a little as the faint night breeze played across her bare shoulders. Daniel sat down behind her, pulling her into the V of his legs so that she could lean back against his chest, and he wrapped his arms around her from behind.

"Warmer?"

Antonia nodded. She felt, in fact, just about perfect, surrounded by Daniel's heat, the taste of champagne in her mouth, its buoyancy infectious.

"Thank you for coming with me," Daniel went on after a moment. "I mean it. It made the evening a lot easier to bear."

"Thank you for taking me," Antonia responded promptly. "I enjoyed it. It was my first prom."

"Your first? You didn't go in high school?"

"We didn't have one. I went to one of those oh-so-First-Four-Hundred-Families—"

Daniel's eyebrows rose and he grinned. "First Four Whats?"

"First Four Hundred. The original families to populate Virginia—that's the big thing there, like coming over on the Mayflower if you live in Massachusetts."

"And here I thought we were a big deal for moving in here two generations ago."

"Hardly. My mother can tell you all about ancestors who lived four hundred years ago in such detail that you'd think she knew them. It's tedious, believe me. Anyway, the thing is, it was an all-girls' school. We didn't have anything so plebeian—or fun—as a prom. We never had anything where you could bring a date because one never knew what kind of riffraff some 'misguided' girl might bring to it. So every year we had two dances—one in the fall and one in the spring."

"And what did you girls do? Dance with each other?"

Antonia chuckled at the thought. "No. That would probably have shocked the board even more. No, we allowed an all-boys' academy—of appropriate social status, of course—to be bussed over to the school, and we could dance with them. It was a terrible ordeal, really, except for a very few girls who actually had something going on with some of the boys from Beauford Prep. It was straight out of the fifties. I always spent the entire evening sitting against the wall."

"You? I find that hard to believe."

"It's the truth."

"Why? Was Beauford Prep a school for the blind?'

Antonia chuckled. "Thank you. But, no, they could see perfectly well. I was taller than almost every boy there, and I was shy and stiff. It was an absolutely miserable experience.''

''Sounds it. Well, maybe you were able to fend off the boredom tonight by watching how the other half lives.''

''Don't be classist. And it wasn't boring. I enjoyed watching all those kids, so bright and hopeful.''

''So without a clue.'' Daniel groaned.

''But that's the whole point of life, isn't it? Not knowing what's going to happen? Just plunging in and dealing with it as it comes. Makes it exciting.''

''That's true. But sometimes I think that I could have done with a little less excitement.''

''Mmm. Maybe.'' She wondered if his sentiments had been prompted by the memories of his own prom that this one must have brought back. He had surely gone to his high school prom with Lurleen. Antonia was faintly surprised at the little stab of pain that went through her at the thought that Daniel might have spent this evening in bittersweet memories of his first wife and their prom, rather than enjoying the odd, piquant situation as she had. Had he been remembering the things he and Lurleen had done, the way their lives had gone, the pain of their divorce?

''Did tonight remind you of your prom?'' she asked, even though she was not at all sure she wanted to hear his answer.

''A little. It's not the same. They've built a new high school. It's not the old one where I went to school. And the music and everything's so different. But the feeling's familiar. I guess you don't lose that. You know—that young and totally sure and totally insecure at the same time kind of feeling. But I had more fun at the one tonight.''

‘‘You did?'' Antonia was so amazed that she sat up straight and turned around to look into his face. ‘‘Why? I figured you went with James's mother, and you had one of those magical sort of nights. You know…''

Daniel grimaced. ‘‘Oh, we had one of our nights, all right, but I wouldn't call it magical. We had a big fight right in the middle of the dance floor. Lurleen went off and stayed in the girls' bathroom half the night, and I had to send two or three different girls in to coax her out. She finally came out, but she stayed mad at me for three days.''

‘‘Why?''

He shrugged. ‘‘I don't remember now. Lurleen had kind of a hot temper. Probably it was about her leaving town. She always wanted to get away from Angel Eye. I should have listened, of course, but I was too bull-headed. I figured I could make her so happy she wouldn't want to leave here. Love conquers all, and all that kind of thing.'' He let out a humorless chuckle. ‘‘I was a pretty sappy guy.''

‘‘No. Not sappy. You sound like a very sweet guy.''

‘‘However you want to put it, I was wrong. We got married and had a kid right off, and she still wanted to get out of Angel Eye. Three years later, she lit out.''

Antonia could hear the faint thread of pain in his voice even after all these years, and the sound started up an odd little ache in her chest. ‘‘I'm sorry.''

‘‘Don't be. I was stupid. Lurleen and I never be-longed together. We weren't alike, didn't want the same things, didn't think the same...the only time we got along was in bed. That's what love can't conquer—the fact that the two of you don't belong together. We were better off apart, and I guess, in the long run, James was better off, too.''

''If you could go back to then and know what was going to happen, would you change what you did? Do it differently?''

''I'm not sure.'' Daniel was a quiet for a moment, then said, ''No, I don't think so. I wouldn't have James if I had taken a different path. Despite all the rest of it, I couldn't give him up. What about you?''

''Yeah, I think I probably would. I would have done what I wanted, gone to vet school after I finished college. But, then, maybe I would have turned out a different person, someone I wouldn't like as well. Maybe I'd still be trying to please my parents.''

''You know, this is way too serious,'' Daniel said, reaching over and picking up the champagne bottle to refill their glasses. ''We're here to celebrate. Have some more champagne.''

''All right.'' Antonia held out her glass to be filled. *Daniel was right. This was no time to be sitting around picking over their past lives. The evening had been too good to ruin it that way.*

She took another sip of the champagne and looked out into the night. The moon was hovering just over a distant mesa now, huge and white and incredibly romantic. Her past seemed very far away at this moment, almost as if it had happened to another person. It felt so good, sitting in the circle of Daniel's arms, the night breeze playing softly over her skin. *So what if Daniel had loved his first wife to distraction? The important thing was that he was here with her now.*

She felt the velvet brush of Daniel's lips at the juncture of her neck and shoulders, and she closed her eyes, luxuriating in the sheer pleasure of it. His mouth trailed slowly up the side of her neck, exposed by her elegant upswept hairdo, until he reached her earlobe. Gently he took the lobe between his teeth and teased it, sending erotic shivers throughout her. His hand began to move over her body, sliding up over her stomach until it reached her breast. He lingered there, gently caressing the full orb and cupping it, sliding his thumb over the hardening bud of her nipple.

Antonia could feel herself melting inside, her loins softening with the heat of desire. Daniel moved on to her other breast, arousing it in the same way. He kissed his way back down the side of her neck and out across her shoulder, and his hand glided up over her chest, hooking under the strap of her dress and pushing it down over her shoulder so that it hung looped over her arm. He pressed his lips against the point of her shoulder. She could feel his breath, hot and moist, against her skin. His tongue came out to taste her flesh, and she shivered as the sensation went through her like electricity, turning her insides aching and warm.

As his mouth worked its way back along her collarbone, he slipped his hand down beneath the top of her dress. The material fell away easily, and his hand drifted over her breast, exploring the tender flesh. Antonia drew in a sharp breath at his touch. Her breasts grew full and aching under his caresses, the nipples tightening into hard buttons. He played with them, gently pressing and releasing, pulling, circling, until desire was pounding in her, heightened by the velvety nibbling of his lips on her shoulders and neck.

Antonia made a low sound, arching back against him. He responded by burying his lips in her neck, both his hands roaming her body hungrily. She half-turned toward him, and he twisted to meet her, his hand coming up to the side of her head, holding it in place as he kissed her thoroughly and deeply. Antonia moaned, her hands curling into the lapels of his jacket and holding on, as if she might fly apart otherwise. She could not remember another man's kiss that had stirred her like this, that had excited, confused and overwhelmed her senses so fiercely. She trembled as she kissed him back, her hands coming up and sinking into his thick hair.

She caressed his scalp and neck, sliding down to his broad shoulders. His jacket frustrated her exploration, and with an impatient noise, she slipped her hands between their bodies, laying them flat against his shirt and sliding up and out beneath his tux jacket, exploring the hard lines of bone and muscle through his shirt.

It was not enough. She wanted to be naked against him, to feel his skin beneath her fingertips, searing hot with passion. She wanted to explore every inch of him, to taste and caress and tease into a frenzy—all the while feeling him doing the very same things to her. In that moment, she knew that she would not be satisfied until she had him inside her, filling her, pushing the limits of their desire.

She wanted him right here, right now, yet even as

his hand slid down over her hip and onto her leg, caressing her through the soft gown, she knew that was impossible. She could not make love to him for the first time on this bony outcropping of rock, scrambling out of their formal clothes, as frantic and irresponsible as any teenagers after the prom. That was not the way she was, not the way she wanted to live. No matter how desire tore at her, she had won wisdom and maturity after a long, hard-fought battle, and she was not going to throw it out the window just because all her nerves were standing on end and screaming for more.

"Wait," she said, and when the word came out soft and weak, she pulled back, clearing her throat and saying it again. "Wait. No."

His body remained taut as a bowstring for a moment, his muscles hard and tensed. Then he let out a sigh and forcibly relaxed. His arms loosened around her. "I'm sorry. I choose the most inopportune times and places, don't I?"

"It's lovely and romantic, but..." She pulled away, turning and shrugging back into the straps of her dress.

The breeze was cool against her heated skin without the enveloping protection of his arms, and Antonia would have liked to have gone back into his embrace. But she set her jaw and reminded herself that her mind was in control of what she did, not her animal instincts. It was her instincts and desires, her emotions, that had gotten her into the mess of her marriage years ago, and she was determined never to let those things run her life again.

"But it's not very practical," she finished, wrapping

her arms around herself to combat the night chill that had fallen here on the edge of the desert. She felt a trifle guilty and even a little worried that her rejection would make Daniel dislike her, but she suppressed the feelings as she had learned to make herself do, reminding herself that she had the right to make her own decisions.

Daniel sighed. "Yeah, no doubt you're right." He shrugged out of his tux jacket and laid it around her shoulders. "Sorry. I really didn't bring you up here for a seduction scene. I just wanted to show you the place." His mouth quirked into a grin. "Somehow, around you, I seem to get carried away. You want another glass of champagne?"

Antonia smiled back, relief trickling through her at Daniel's easy acceptance. "Maybe a little."

He poured out more for both of them, and they sat, carefully not touching, and talked, leaning back to look up at the night sky. Sometime later they left, folding up the blanket and carrying it and the champagne back to the truck. Daniel drove Antonia home and walked her to her front door.

"How about next Friday we'll go on a real date?" Daniel suggested. "No kids. Dinner and a movie in Hammond or something like that?"

"Sounds nice."

He left her with a light kiss on the mouth, and Antonia went inside. She turned on the lights and walked into her bedroom, doing a little twirl as she went, just for fun. The telephone rang, and a little thrill of alarm shot through her. She stood for a moment, frozen, looking at it.

Then she narrowed her eyes and set her jaw and strode across the room to the phone on her bedside table. "Hello?"

There was the same silence on the other end. Irritation swept her. *She was not going to let some idiot, least of all Alan, ruin this evening.*

"Get a life," she snapped, and slammed the receiver down.

Chapter 7

Antonia leaned back in her chair and rolled her head from one side to the other. She laid down the pen and clenched and unclenched her hand. It had been a long, hard day, and she had only now, at almost seven-thirty, finished writing up the notes for the surgery she had just performed on Homer Harris's bay gelding, who had somehow or other run into a steel fence post and opened up his side. It hadn't helped any that she hadn't gotten to sleep last night until almost three o'clock in the morning. That was the fourth time this week that she had been unable to go to sleep when she went to bed, and every time it happened, it just got worse and she got more irritable, until she was getting to where she dreaded seeing night approach.

With a sigh, she stood up and took off her lab coat. She wondered what she might have in the fridge to eat. She didn't want to go by the grocery store or drop in to the Moonstone. But she certainly had no inclination to cook tonight. She was weary to the bone.

It was those damn calls.

Antonia's mouth twitched in irritation. She had had three more of them this week, and it had worn her nerves thin. She told herself that it was not Alan, that he didn't know her number or even where she was. She reminded herself that playing silly phone tricks was a favorite among middle school children, and that, moreover, there was not much for a child to do in a little town like Angel Eye, and the restiveness of spring had probably set in. Lots of people got hang-up calls, and though she had received too many of them to write it off as coincidence, it did not mean that her ex-husband was after her.

That was what she told herself. What she felt was an entirely different matter. Every time she received a call, she was thrown back into the days after she had left Alan, when he had harassed her with just such phone calls at all hours of the day and night, culminating in his finding her alone and beating her unconscious. She could not keep from remembering the terror that had accompanied her out of her marriage, the shaky uncertainty that perhaps he was right and she never would be able to escape him, no matter what she did. And no matter how much she reminded herself that she was a different person now—stronger, more capable, no longer frightened and insecure—just the thought of that time still had the power to turn her to jelly inside.

She had stopped answering her phone, letting the answering machine take the calls, but she had found that that strategy did little to ease her tension. Whenever the phone rang now, she went to stand beside the answering machine, every nerve on edge, listening for the silence, the click, letting out her breath when it was someone she knew on the other end leaving a message, but going even tauter when the silence stretched out. She had even thought about changing her number to an unlisted one, but that was scarcely practical for a vet in a small town. People depended on her; they had to be able to reach her.

Her stomach rumbled with hunger as she picked up her purse and started down the hall, turning off the lights. Just as she reached the side hall, where she would turn to go out to her car, there was a noise behind her. She jumped and turned around, her heart pounding. She saw nothing in the clinic behind her, dimly lit by the fading sun coming in through the windows at the front. She stood still, watching.

A knock sounded at the front door, and she let out a little shriek, all her nerves screaming. She forced herself to relax, drawing a deep breath. It wasn't the boogie man, for pity's sake, she told herself, and made her feet start toward the front of the clinic. No doubt it was simply someone with an animal emergency who had come to the clinic hoping to find them still open.

A trifle unsteadily, she walked toward the front. A large form loomed up suddenly before one of the front windows, and Antonia flinched and stopped again, swallowing hard. The man put his hands up to the window, cupping them around his eyes and peering in.

"Antonia?" She heard the flat Texas accent, muffled by the glass, and in that instant she recognized him.

''Daniel?'' Relief flooded her, and she hurried to the front door and pulled it open. ''Daniel?''

''Hey.'' He turned to the door, smiling tentatively.

He looked unbelievably good, she thought, tall and broad-shouldered in jeans and a sports jacket over a white shirt. His jeans were dark blue, almost new-looking, and the tooled leather boots were shined to a mirror gloss. Even the cowboy hat on his head was not the straw one he usually wore, but a soft felt one.

He took off the hat now, politely saying, ''Sorry. Are you busy? I wasn't sure what to do. You weren't home, so I thought I'd check and see if you had gotten caught at the clinic.''

Antonia stared at him blankly for a moment, before understanding struck her like a thunderbolt and she gasped. ''Oh, no! Is this Friday?''

He nodded, his eyebrows going up quizzically. ''Forget about our date tonight?''

''Yes. I mean, no, I didn't forget our date.'' She could feel herself beginning to flush furiously. ''I lost track of what day it was. It seemed like Thursday to-day, and then we had such a workload, I kind of lost track of everything. Oh, dear, I am so sorry. I feel terrible. You must think I'm awful.''

Daniel grinned. ''Nah. Could happen to anybody. Rough day, huh?''

''The worst.'' Unconsciously Antonia sagged. ''I'm sorry. Here, let me lock the door.''

She turned back to the door she had just closed and began to search through her purse for her keys. As she did so, she felt Daniel's hands come up to her shoulders, and he kneaded the taut muscles beneath her skin. Antonia let out a little moan of pure pleasure as some of the tension began to ooze away.

"That feels wonderful."

He chuckled as his thumbs dug into her muscles. "Good. Believe me, I know how sore muscles feel. What happened?"

"One crisis after another. First Mrs. Kritzer came in with that damned Lhasa who always tries to bite me."

"Buster?" Daniel let out a laugh. "That dog bit Quinn once when he went over there to answer a call, and you'd have thought Quinn was the one who'd hurt the dog, the way Mrs. Kritzer acted."

"I'm sure. Rita says he terrorizes the neighborhood."

"Yeah. But not half as much as Mrs. Kritzer does."

Antonia chuckled. Having been under the old woman's gimlet gaze, she could well understand how a neighborhood could quake in fear of the old woman.

"She was certain that Buster had been poisoned. In fact, it turned out that he had gotten into a bunch of candy and eaten himself sick." She turned the key in both locks, securing the front door, and turned around somewhat reluctantly—the kneading of Daniel's strong hands had felt unbelievably wonderful. "Thank you. That helped a great deal. You're very good at that."

"I aim to please," he replied.

Antonia smiled, enjoying the way his dark eyes twinkled down at her. "I'm sorry. I guess I've ruined our evening. If I went home and changed right now, I'm afraid we wouldn't be able to make a movie in Hammond."

Daniel shrugged. "Don't worry about it. I'm not that big on movies, anyway, as James will be happy to tell you. And you've probably already seen it in Houston, since you've only been here a couple of months. Hammond doesn't exactly get first-run movies."

"Probably not. I'm really not all that big on movies, either."

They stood for a moment looking at each other. Antonia wished she hadn't forgotten what day it was. She had been looking forward all week to going out with him, and here she had spoiled it.

"But, you know, the evening's not ruined, really..." Daniel went on hesitantly. "I mean, unless you're too tired. We could still go out for dinner in Hammond. Or we could stop by the store and get a couple of steaks. I could grill them for you." He smiled. "I'd rub your back some more."

"Now that seals the deal," Antonia responded lightly, although the thought of him massaging her back in the privacy of her home almost took her breath away.

After a short discussion, they agreed that Daniel would go buy the steaks and drop by the video store, while Antonia went home to change. Antonia was grateful for the extra time and suspected that Daniel had suggested going to the video store just to give her a few extra minutes to get ready. Fortunately, she didn't have to pick up much to make the house look presentable. The cat, of course, demanded feeding immediately, but after that she was able to take a speedy shower and get dressed before Daniel arrived. She curled her wet hair up into a knot atop her head and even managed to put on a touch of lipstick, blush and mascara before he rang the doorbell. That would have to do, she thought, glancing at herself in the mirror. She had put on a simple blue sundress with a flattering halter neckline, and it did nice things for both her figure and the color of her eyes.

From the way Daniel's eyes drifted involuntarily down her body when she opened the door, she had to assume that he thought the dress was flattering, also. She smiled, realizing that she felt a great deal less weary than she had when she left the clinic. *It was amazing what a little open admiration did for a person's spirits.*

Antonia led him into the kitchen, and he set down the brown paper bag on the counter. He reached inside and pulled out three plastic video cases. "Didn't know what you'd like, so I got a selection. Charlene at the video store said women liked them." He glanced at them somewhat doubtfully. "'Course, she also said everybody died in this one, so I don't know how much fun that one is."

"I'm sure I'll like any of them," Antonia said, taking the videos from his hand.

He looked somewhat aghast when he discovered that she had no outdoor barbecue upon which to grill the steaks, but he made do with her stove. She put potatoes in the microwave and cut up a salad for them while he cooked the steaks, and before long they were able to sit down to a hearty dinner. Mitzi had decided that she worshiped Daniel and came to sit next to his chair throughout the meal. Antonia had the sneaking suspicion that Daniel was slipping her little bits of the steak.

Afterwards, they sat down on the couch in the living room to watch one of the three movies, a romantic comedy. The cat followed them and insisted on sitting in Daniel's lap, and finally Antonia had to close her in the kitchen. For a time Mitzi serenaded them with a series of moans worthy of an animal that was being killed, but finally she stopped. Antonia could picture her turning a haughty shoulder and stalking over to her cat bed for the rest of the evening.

Daniel looped his arm around Antonia's shoulders, and it seemed only natural to curl up against his side. They talked and laughed as they watched the movie, comfortable together, yet also always aware of an underlying current of attraction between them. For the first time in days Antonia felt completely relaxed and without a thought about her ex or the mysterious phone calls she had been receiving.

Once she shifted position, straightening out her legs, and Daniel reached down and swung her feet up into his lap. He slipped off her sandals and began to massage her feet, and Antonia promptly lost the thread of what was going on in the movie.

His firm touch eased away the tension in her as well as soothing her feet, tired from a day spent standing. Antonia could feel knots in her shoulders and neck loosening, draining away the last remnants of her stressful week.

At the same time, however, his skillful fingers elicited an equally strong reaction in her that had nothing to do with stress or tiredness. A low sexual tension began to throb between the two of them, growing slowly. She was aware of the sensuality of his skin against hers, his warmth seeping into her, the tingling response to his touch zigzagging up into the rest of her body. She wanted to stretch languidly, to rub her other foot against his leg, to tease and entice him as he was subtly enticing her.

His fingers worked their magic on her feet until Antonia was almost melting. She wondered if he realized the reaction he was eliciting from her. He turned, and his eyes met hers, hot and charged with energy, and she realized that the same fire burned in him. They looked at each other for a long moment. His hand slid slowly up her foot and onto her ankle. Antonia shivered as his hand moved higher, the rough calluses of his palm rasping over her soft skin. He leaned closer, fire lighting his dark eyes.

At that moment the telephone shrilled beside Antonia on the end table. She jumped, a shriek escaping her lips. She stared at Daniel for a moment, frozen. Then she jumped to her feet and grabbed the receiver.

"Hello?" Her voice came out hoarse. Her heart was pounding crazily, her nerves jangling.

"Antonia?" a woman's voice said hesitantly.

"Rita. Oh. Thank God."

"Antonia? Are you all right? What's the matter?"

She realized then how odd her words must have sounded to Rita—not to mention Daniel, who was looking at her with a faint frown forming on his brow.

Antonia forced out a little laugh. "I'm sorry. The phone just scared me, that's all. I was—I was watching a movie."

Antonia glanced at the television screen as she said the words and noticed that the end credits were crawling down the screen. She had no idea how the movie had ended; she had been too involved in what Daniel was doing to her. She could feel a blush rising in her cheeks.

"What kind of a Friday night is that, girl?" Rita asked. "You should be out having fun."

"I'm too tired," Antonia responded. "That surgery today really took it out of me."

"Yeah. It was rough. Then when I got home—"

She could hear Rita settling in for a long talk on the other end of the line, and Antonia's heart sank. She could not chat with her friend with Daniel sitting on the couch. But if she let Rita know that Daniel was there with her, the news would be all over the gossip circuit before the next morning. She shifted, casting a glance at Daniel. He was leaning back, arms stretched across the top of the couch, watching her. She could not tell what he was thinking. *Had he found her reaction to the phone's ringing peculiar? Or would he put it down to her having been lost in the sensuality of the moment?* Either way, she supposed, it was embarrassing.

"Uh, listen, Rita," she said, cutting in the first time Rita paused in her description of her children's misdemeanors that evening. "I have to, ah—there's something on the stove. Could I call you back later?"

"Sure," Rita replied easily. "Any time. Unfortunately, we're not going anywhere tonight."

Antonia hung up and turned back to Daniel a little awkwardly. "I'm sorry. That was Rita Delgado. I didn't want to say you were here...."

"Wise choice." Daniel paused, then said, "Antonia...the way you looked when the phone rang..."

Antonia gave him a bright smile. "You must think I'm silly, the way I jumped. I wasn't expecting the phone to ring, and it startled me."

"Yeah, me, too. But...I don't know, you looked scared. Is something wrong?"

Antonia made a face. "I've just been getting these stupid phone calls. It's nothing."

His brow furrowed. "What kind of phone calls?"

"I don't know. Maybe there's just something wrong with my phone. I haven't checked it out, really. It's probably just some kids playing pranks. I've gotten several calls where nobody said anything. There was just silence. They're kind of spooky."

"Did you tell the phone company? Maybe you ought to change your number. Get an unlisted one."

"I can't, because of the clinic," she explained. "My patients have to be able to get hold of me."

"You could make arrangements. People could call the clinic and you could have the calls forwarded here. Use one of those beeper things and call people back."

"I don't—I don't want to tell anyone. Anyway, I'm sure it's nothing."

Daniel's frown deepened. "I don't think it's something you ought to blow off. People do some crazy things these days."

"Somebody besides me probably wouldn't even think anything about it." Antonia sat down on the couch. She looked at him and sighed. He looked so concerned, so solid and strong, that she found herself wanting to tell him all about it. The urge startled her. She almost never talked about Alan to anyone; she had told no one in Angel Eye about him, even Rita.

"It's happened to you before?" Daniel guessed.

Antonia nodded. "When I got divorced. My ex-husband used to call me and do that, not say anything, just sit there for a while and then hang up."

"Sounds like a jerk."

"He was."

They sat for a moment. Antonia could feel Daniel watching her. Finally he asked, "Was he more of a jerk than that?"

Antonia nodded. Tears flooded her eyes, surprising her, and she blinked them away. "Oh, yeah. A lot more."

Daniel curled his arm around her shoulders and gently pulled her to him. Antonia laid her head on his shoulder, snuggling against his side. It felt so good there, so safe and warm, that she wanted to rest like that forever.

"Did he hit you?" he asked in a low voice.

Antonia nodded, and Daniel's arm tightened around her. She felt his lips brush her hair, and something seemed to give way inside her. She began to cry, tears streaming down her face. It had been a long time since she had cried about Alan and her marriage. But now she found the story tumbling out, jumbled and rushed and interspersed with tears. She wanted to stop. She knew how awful she must look, red-faced and swollen-eyed. But she could not seem to stem the flow of words. She told him everything, too embarrassed to look him in the face, but desperate to get it out—the beatings, Alan's vitriolic criticisms and sarcasm that had crushed her self-confidence almost as much as his physical violence, the harassment he had subjected her to when she filed for divorce. It all spilled out, until finally she wound down, exhausted and spent, but peaceful.

She sat for a long moment, her head still on Daniel's chest, listening to the steady beat of his heart, feeling his chest rise and fall beneath her cheek. She thought about the things she had told him, things she had related to almost no one besides her therapist, and she wondered if she had ruined any possibility of a relationship between them. It wouldn't surprise her, she mused, if he rose now, giving some reason why he had to return home, and she never saw him again.

"I'm sorry," he said finally, his voice husky, and his hand slid up and down her back in a slow, soothing motion. "I wish he was here right now. I'd put that sorry son of a bitch out of his misery."

Antonia let out a watery little chuckle. "I don't think *he* was in misery, just anyone who lived with him."

"They put him in jail?"

Antonia shook her head. "No. I didn't file charges. It was part of the divorce settlement we worked out. His lawyer convinced him not to contest the divorce and put me through a trial, and I agreed not to prosecute him for putting me in the hospital." She sighed.

''It was cowardly of me. I should have helped them put him away. What if he's hurt other women since then? But my lawyer said Alan wouldn't get much, if any, jail time—probably probation considering the fact that he'd never been arrested and that he was this 'fine, upstanding citizen.' A fellow lawyer. I couldn't bear the thought of two trials, of having to face him and testify against him.''

A shudder ran through her even now at the thought. ''I just couldn't do it,'' she added in a low voice.

''Of course not. You had been through too much. You're not a coward.''

''Yeah, I am,'' Antonia said a little bitterly, sitting up and pulling away from him. ''If I weren't a coward, I would have left him a long time before I did. I wouldn't have married him, probably.''

''You knew he was abusive before you got married?''

''No. But I should have seen the signs.''

''Hard to see warning signs when you're knee-deep in love,'' Daniel pointed out. ''I know. I've been there.''

''There must have been some weakness in me that attracted him to me,'' Antonia went on, voicing thoughts she had gone over a hundred times before. ''He knew somehow that he could control me. Abuse me. I just didn't realize it.''

''I don't buy that,'' Daniel said flatly. ''That's blaming the victim for getting victimized. It's like somebody saying, 'Oh, I shouldn't have had that nice TV set, 'cause then the burglar wouldn't have been tempted to break in and steal it.' I feel sure that what attracted him was the way you looked, not some intangible weakness in you. He looked at you and saw a gorgeous woman that he wanted. So he hid the way he really was, and courted you and got you to marry him. Then he set out to control you, because he was a sick bastard. And those things are not your fault. You couldn't keep from being beautiful and desirable any more than you can keep from being smart. If there's anything you should be kicking yourself about, it's having the bad luck to marry the weasel."

Antonia smiled. Her therapist had assured her over and over that it was not her fault, and she had learned to believe it—in her head. Yet she had never quite been able to get rid of the niggling little doubt deep inside that somehow there was something wrong in her that had attracted Alan or somehow set him off. Moreover, she suspected that other people thought the same thing. It was warming to hear Daniel's down-to-earth denial of it—and somehow more reassuring than any psychological reasoning had been. "Believe me, I do kick myself about that."

"You think this is him on the phone?" Daniel asked after a moment.

"That's the thing—I honestly don't know." Antonia sighed. "That was the first thing I thought of—that Alan was doing it again. But I can't tell. Whoever it is doesn't say a word. I can't hear anything, even breathing. For all I know, it could be a prank—or a problem with my phone line."

"You can find that out real easily. Just call the phone company and have them check for problems. And I can call Quinn, see what he can do."

Antonia shook her head. "That's okay." It would be wonderfully easy to turn the whole thing over to him, but she couldn't do that. She had to handle this herself. She had worked too hard at getting her independence to hand it all over to a man now, no matter how nice and helpful he was.

Antonia looked over at Daniel. He looked strong and implacable and incredibly good to her. She realized how much she wanted to go back into his arms again. For a moment she resisted the impulse, but then she gave in and leaned once more against his side. His arm curved naturally around her, and she snuggled into him, breathing in his scent, feeling the firm strength of his chest beneath her. Her eyes, heavy-lidded from crying, drifted closed. It was so easy being with him this way, she thought, so warm and comfortable....

Antonia blinked, coming awake. The television was off, and the lights in the room cast a soft yellow glow. She was lying on the sofa, resting against Daniel's chest. She had a faint headache, but she felt calm and peaceful inside, almost happy. It took a moment for her to remember what had happened. She looked up at Daniel, slightly embarrassed.

"Hi."

"Hi there." He smiled down at her. "Sorry. I didn't mean to wake you. My arm sort of fell asleep, and I was trying to move it around."

"Oh, no. I should apologize to you," Antonia said, sitting up. She didn't really like the way it felt to move away from Daniel's arms, and the thought unsettled her. "I can't believe I fell asleep like that."

"You had a rough day," he reminded her. "I didn't mind."

"You must have been terribly bored. How long have I been asleep?"

"About an hour, I guess. I wasn't bored. I looked at the news a little, and sat here and thought." He cocked an eyebrow at her. "I'm just a boring kind of guy, I guess." He ran a gentle hand over her hair, down her back. "I liked watching you sleep."

Antonia felt a little breathless at his both his words and his touch. The warmth inside her grew and changed, no longer safe and sweet, but charged with sexual energy. An ache started low in her abdomen, throbbing and insistent. Just looking at him, she could feel her whole body softening and opening to him. Involuntarily she leaned toward him, turning her face up to his.

Daniel needed no further invitation. He bent and kissed her, his mouth settling on hers with a sigh of satisfaction. He had been thinking about kissing her for the last hour, feeling her sleep in his arms. It had been pleasure and pain to hold her like that, heat building unsatisfied inside him even as he enjoyed the soft warmth of her body in his arms, trusting and vulnerable. Now that heat came flooding out in his kiss, igniting an answering flame in Antonia. The desire that had been between them earlier, before the telephone call, sprang into life again, consuming them with its fire.

Her lips clung to his, almost desperate in their intensity, and she wrapped her arms around his neck, pressing her body into his. He could feel her breasts against his chest, the nipples pointing and eager. Hunger roared through him, mingling with the gentler delight of holding her. He wanted to protect her; he also wanted to take her, to plunge deep inside her and make her his own.

His hands went to her waist and slid upward, cupping her full breasts. Antonia moaned low in her throat at the touch of his fingers on her sensitive flesh. She wanted to feel them on her bare skin, without the barrier of her clothes between them. She reached up and unfastened the tie of her halter, letting the sides fall apart and slide down her body. Daniel took advantage of the invitation she offered, moving his hands beneath the cloth and curving them around her bare breasts. He squeezed and caressed her, desire pounding in him like a jackhammer.

Daniel pulled back, his breath rasping in his throat. "No. I shouldn't."

"What?" Antonia looked at him, dazed and uncertain. "What do you mean?"

"You're—I—it would be taking advantage of—the situation. You know. Taking advantage of the fact that you're vulnerable."

Even as he spoke, he could not keep his eyes from roaming over her—taking in the tumbled state of her hair, which had come loose as she slept; her lips, soft and swollen from their passionate kisses; her breasts, bared by the fallen cloth of her dress, white and full, centered by desire-hardened nipples—and his desire pulsed hotter within him.

Antonia looked at him for a moment, then smiled provocatively. ''Go ahead,'' she said, standing and reaching back to unzip the lower part of her dress. It drifted down to the floor in a heap, leaving her clad in only a lacy wisp of panties. ''I want you to take advantage of me.''

He gazed at her, stunned, for another moment, then reached out and pulled her down onto his lap.

Chapter 8

They kissed again and again, unable to slake their passion, as his hands roamed over her near-naked body. He caressed her breasts and stomach, delving under the flimsy material of her underwear to caress her rounded buttocks. He explored the wonderfully long expanse of her legs, coming back up the inside of her thigh to cup the center of her femininity, heated and damp, throbbing with desire for him. She moaned as he touched her there, and he slipped a finger beneath the material, stroking and exploring, driving them both into a frenzy of passion that was almost unbearable in its intensity.

Daniel stood, picking Antonia up in his arms, and carried her through the living room and down the hall to her bedroom, thanking Fate that the house was small enough that he did not have to search for it. He stopped dead still at the door to the bedroom, another jolt of pure sexual hunger rushing through him.

The no-nonsense Antonia had given in to all her feminine, sensual instincts here in this intimate room. The wooden floor gleamed with a golden glow, softened by a plush white rug beside the bed. The bed was high, with four posts and a tester frame running around the top. White mosquito netting fell in a froth from the tester, delicate and pure, matching the white comforter that covered the bed. It was a sensual setting, enticing in its purity and softness.

Daniel set Antonia down on her feet, swallowing to ease the sudden dryness in his throat. He looked at her, knowing that there wasn't a force in the world at this moment that could keep him from getting into that bed with this woman. He could not speak, his chest rising and falling like a bellows, but the heat in his eyes spoke his intention very clearly.

Antonia felt that heat all through her as his eyes bored into hers. The sheer force of his hunger was almost as powerful an aphrodisiac as his kisses had been. She could feel desire flooding between her legs. Her breasts swelled and tingled, the tips aching for the feel of his skin, his mouth, upon them. She wanted to wrap her legs around him, feel him inside her, filling her. Her knees began to tremble. She held out her arms to him.

Daniel couldn't get out of his clothes fast enough. Yanking off his boots, fumbling at his buttons, tugging, jerking, shoving, he removed his clothes in a frenzy, all the while kissing and caressing her. Antonia laughed and pushed him away, helping to tug his shirt off his arms and down, and unfastening his belt as she walked backward, pulling him gently along. He went with her eagerly, thwarting her efforts by stopping to pull her into his arms and kiss her long and deeply.

Finally she came up against the bed and tumbled back on it. She lay there, looking up at him, and Daniel stood for a moment, gazing at her, taking in the beautiful picture she made lying against the feminine white cover. Then he reached down and pulled the triangle of lace down and off her legs. He stepped out of his own jeans and climbed onto the bed after her.

He did not slide between her legs immediately, as he ached to do. Instead, he lay down beside her, propping himself up on one elbow, and began to caress her body with his other hand. Lazily he explored her flesh, discovering each pleasure point and dwelling on it until Antonia was writhing with delight. His mouth followed his skilled fingertips, kissing and nuzzling. He kissed his way down to the peak of each breast, then circled the tip with his tongue until the bud was hard and pointing and Antonia was arching up beneath him, digging her heels into the bed. Then, finally, he pulled the nipple into his mouth, suckling and caressing until Antonia was almost wild with hunger, panting and begging for release.

Then, and only then, did he at last move between her legs and thrust into her. Antonia gasped at the pleasure, moving her hips against him. He groaned, his hands digging into her hips, and began to move inside her. Thrusting and retreating, he stoked their passion, pushing them higher and higher, until at last they burst in a glorious explosion of pleasure, drifting down into a blissful, scattered peace.

Antonia awoke early the next morning, brought to consciousness by the sun slanting through the window where she had not thought to close the curtain. Her eyes felt swollen and puffy, and the sun pierced them, starting up a low headache. She started to roll over to turn away from the sun, and it was then that she realized a man's heavy arm was draped over her shoulders, weighing her down. Daniel!

Her heart began to pound as she remembered everything that had happened the night before. It occurred to her that perhaps she had made a terrible mistake. This was moving much too fast. She barely knew the man. *What would he think of her?* She remembered how she had cried and told him all about Alan and her marriage, and she blushed. She rarely told anyone about that period of her life; it shamed her that she had let the man rule her life so completely. She had never revealed it to anyone who she knew as little as she knew Daniel Sutton.

She would have to explain to him that she didn't usually act this way, that she had slipped, given in to a moment of unusual emotional turmoil. She could tell him that she had to take a step backward, review the situation, make sure that she was doing the right, intelligent thing....

Yet even in the midst of her panic, she also felt again the way her chest had eased as she told him and he held her, his arms warm and strong and steady around her. Her body was still warm and relaxed, too, melted by their lovemaking. The blush in her cheeks increased as she thought about the abandoned way she had responded to his touch, how she had wrapped her arms around him and moved against him in passionate joy. At just the thought, her loins warmed involuntarily, and she realized that even as she was stabbed by anxiety at what she had done the night before, she was wanting him all over again, recalling the primitive satisfaction that had invaded her body last night.

It occurred to Antonia that the Texas sun had addled her brain. She was usually so steady, so logical, practical, unemotional; it was one of her tenets for the past four years that she never let a man disturb her equilibrium. Yet here she was feeling as jittery, unsure and confused as a teenager.

She began to move cautiously, wriggling to get out from under his arm. She stopped abruptly, heat flooding her as she felt Daniel's unmistakable, unconscious response against her backside.

"No, don't stop now," came Daniel's sleepy voice next to her ear, and he burrowed his face into her hair. "This is just getting good."

He moved his arm, sliding his hand down the front of her naked body, cupping one breast, then caressing her stomach and pressing her hips back into his body. Antonia drew in her breath sharply.

Daniel's lips found her neck, then her ear lobe, and his hand was working magic on the sensitive flesh of her abdomen and breasts.

"Daniel, I—I'm not sure. I mean…uh…ahh…" Her voice came out in a long breath as his fingers delved between her legs, finding the little, pulsing nub of pleasure there.

"Hmm?" His breath was hot against her neck as his mouth trailed down the tender flesh.

"I forget." Pleasure was spreading in hot tendrils all through her now, pushing out the doubts she had felt earlier.

Antonia turned in his arms. In their eager passion last night, she realized, she had not spent nearly enough time on Daniel. She wanted to touch him, to stroke the smooth browned skin stretched over bone and taut muscle, to feel him quiver beneath her hands and mouth.

She put her hands on his chest, then ran them slowly down him. He sucked in a sharp breath, and his skin jumped under her touch. Antonia smiled as she felt the heat surge through his flesh, and she knew that he was as affected by her as she was by him.

"My turn now," she told him with a slow smile. Putting both hands on his chest again, she pushed him back flat on his back and straddled him. She could feel his desire pulsing against her, hot and hard, and she squirmed a little, delighting in the groan that escaped him.

Slowly she explored him, using hands and lips and teeth and tongue. She tasted the salt of his skin, felt the contrasting textures—satin smooth here, rough and callused there—experimented with the ways that she could make him respond, until finally both of them were damp with sweat and breathing as if they'd been in a race, unable to wait any longer for that cataclysmic pleasure that they knew awaited them. But still

Antonia set the pace, taking him into her and moving against him, and he seemed more than content to let her tease and arouse him, digging his fingers into her hips as he held back the furious onslaught of desire that tore at him, until finally her body stiffened and she gasped as wave after wave of fulfillment rocked her. Only then did he let go, allowing his own pleasure to sweep through him in a blinding, red-hot flood.

Afterward, Antonia collapsed against him, spent and trembling, and he wrapped his arms tightly around her. They lay like that for a few minutes, lost in hazy contentment. Suddenly Daniel's arms tightened around her.

"Damn!" he cursed softly, lifting his head and looking toward the window. "It's daylight! What time is it?"

"I don't know," Antonia murmured sleepily, rolling off his chest and onto the bed beside him as he rose up and twisted to look at the clock on her bedside table. "Early. It's Saturday, anyway."

"Yeah, well, maybe that'll mean they'll sleep a little later. Six-oh-five. I might still have a chance."

"A chance of what?" Antonia pushed the hair out of her face and turned to look at him, puzzled. Then her face cleared. "Oh! You mean to get home before James wakes up? Oh dear." She sat up, a worried frown forming between her eyes. "Will he be worried?"

"He probably was just glad last night to see that I wasn't home to see how late *he* got in," Daniel replied candidly. "And this morning, I doubt he'll wake up before noon. Even if he does..." He shrugged. "I don't think he'll worry. He knows I had a date with you last night.''

Antonia quirked an eyebrow. ''So this is common behavior for you on a date?''

Daniel, sliding out of bed and beginning to quickly pull on his clothes, turned to grin at her. A devilish light sparked in his dark eyes. ''Jealous?''

Antonia tossed back her hair, assuming a haughty look that, combined with her modest pose, sheet pulled up to cover her breasts and held with one hand, and her suggestively disheveled state, made Daniel want to crawl right back into bed and begin to kiss her again. ''Of course not,'' she replied with a hint of frost.

''Don't worry. It's not common. But he has eyes. He's got a clue how I feel about you. I don't think he would worry over much about where I was. No—it's your neighbors I'm thinking about.''

''My neighbors? What about them?''

Daniel had finished pulling on his trousers and was now hastily buttoning his shirt while he prowled the room, looking for his boots. ''I don't want them to see my truck out there at this time of the morning. They'll know I spent the night, and that wouldn't help your reputation any.''

Antonia smiled. ''My reputation? Why would anyone care?''

''You're too used to living in Houston, Doc. This is a little country town.'' He found his boots and hurriedly jammed his feet into them. Not bothering to tuck in his shirt, he came back to the bed and leaned over to plant a thorough kiss on her mouth. ''I don't want them gossiping about you.''

His concern warmed Antonia almost as much as his kiss, and she curled her arms around his neck and clung to him for an extra brief moment afterward.

''Hey, darlin', you're going to make it hard to leave if you keep doing that.''

Antonia chuckled and lay back, propping her head on her crossed arms.

''I'll call you.'' He started toward the door, then stopped and turned, looking a little sheepish. ''I mean—if that's okay. If you want me to.''

''Yeah.'' Antonia smiled. ''I want you to.''

Antonia hummed to herself as she drove her SUV toward the clinic. It was Saturday, and while the clinic was open on Saturday mornings as a convenience to their clients, they carried a reduced staff and the doctors took turns manning it. This Saturday was Dr. Carmichael's turn, but Antonia wanted to check on the horse she had operated on the day before, as well as one or two of the other animals whose conditions were rather iffy.

There were a few cars out in front, as it would be another hour before the clinic closed, but Antonia slipped in the side door. She smiled brightly at Rita, who was walking down the hall in the opposite direction, when Rita turned back to look at her.

''Antonia?''

''Yes?'' Antonia tried to school her expression into something bland, but it was difficult to keep the smile from returning to her face.

Rita looked at her speculatively. "What's going on?"

"What do you mean? I'm just here to look at a couple of my animals."

"I don't know. You look...all glow-y." She came a couple of steps closer to Antonia and lowered her voice. "And you never called me back last night. Afterward, I got to thinking about it, and you seemed kind of funny when we were on the phone. Does this have anything to do with a certain horse breeder?"

Antonia lifted her brows. "I can't imagine what you're talking about."

"It does!" Rita exclaimed. "You had a date with him last night, didn't you?"

"I did. Not that it's any of your business."

Rita's eyes grew rounder, and she opened her mouth to speak, then closed it and glanced back toward the room where she was supposed to be. "I've got to get in there or Dr. Carmichael will have a hissy. But don't you go anywhere until I get a chance to talk to you. *¿Comprende?*"

"I understand. But, you know, I do have better things to do with my afternoon than hang around the clinic."

"Like what?"

"I don't know. I thought I would do my nails. Maybe a facial."

"Your nails?" Rita cast an involuntary look at Antonia's nails, cut in a practical manner as short as they could be and utterly unadorned. "The love bug has bitten, that's clear." She pointed a finger at Antonia. "I am through here in thirty minutes. You better not be gone when I get done. Because you and I are going to have lunch afterward, and then we're going to spend a girly afternoon gossiping and facialing.''

''Sounds good to me,'' Antonia responded airily and walked down the hall past Rita toward the double doors leading into the animal pen area. She didn't look back to see Rita staring after her, but she smiled a little to herself.

Rita was waiting for her, purse on her shoulder, when Antonia came back through the double doors to wash up. The rest of the staff had left, except for the technician manning the kennel and pen area.

''Moonstone Café?'' Antonia asked as she began to scrub her hands at the sink.

''Sounds good to me. I called Roberto and told him to take the kids over to Hammond by himself this afternoon.''

''I bet that pleased him.''

Rita shrugged expressively. ''It will do them all good. Bonding with their dad and all that. But not as much good as it will do me to have a girls' afternoon out. Now give. What is going on with you and Daniel Sutton?''

''As if I'd tell you. It'd be all over the county by tomorrow morning.''

''You wound me.'' Rita laid a dramatic hand on her heart. ''I wouldn't tell anything *important*—not if you asked me not to.'' At Antonia's doubtful expression, she added, ''Honestly! Ask anybody. They'll tell you I can keep a secret. I knew Roberto's mom had breast cancer for two weeks before she told anybody else, and I didn't let on a bit.''

''How is Señora Delgado?''

''Sassy as ever. In remission three years now.''

''Good.''

''But the point is, I can keep from telling a soul if I want to. I wouldn't tell anyone all your secrets—at least not the juicy ones.''

''I don't know that there's that much to tell.'' Antonia grinned and added, ''But I like him. A lot. More than I've liked anybody for years.''

''This is great.'' Rita rubbed her hands together with glee. ''So exactly what happened last night?''

Antonia chuckled. ''Now *that* I'm not getting into.''

''Antonia...''

Antonia laughed, shaking her head, as she dried off her hands and started out the door, Rita right on her heels. They drove in separate cars to the Moonstone Café and afterward Rita followed Antonia to her house. Rita had abandoned her efforts to get Antonia to tell her the details of her evening with Daniel, and she settled down to help Antonia indulge in all the girlish sort of activities Antonia usually avoided.

''Are you seeing him again tonight?'' Rita asked as they dabbed on a bright green mask, sitting in front of the mirror in Antonia's bedroom.

''I don't know. He didn't say anything about it. I don't guess so.'' Antonia frowned a little, her happiness marred for the first time that day.

''Don't look like that. I know Daniel Sutton, and there's one thing he is not—fickle. He is definitely not the kind to take you out a time or two and then just disappear.''

''Are you sure?''

''Of course I am. And it's plain as can be that he's smitten. Everybody says so—including his son. Benny told me.''

Her words revived Antonia's spirits, and they were lifted even more a few minutes later when the phone rang and she picked it up to hear Daniel's voice on the other end.

''Hi,'' she said, her voice unconsciously softening and a smile spreading across her lips. Rita grinned and gave her a thumbs-up sign before she thoughtfully left Antonia alone while she went to rummage through Antonia's supply of fingernail polish.

''You know, I was thinking...'' Daniel said without preamble. ''We didn't get that dinner and movie last night, so I wondered...you know, if maybe you'd like to do that this evening instead. I know it's kind of late to call....''

Antonia's smile broadened. ''That sounds nice.''

''Am I being too pushy? I'm pretty rusty with this sort of thing. I just—I was thinking about you, and I wanted to see you again.''

''No, you're not too pushy. I would say you have exactly the right amount of push. I would like to go. Very much.''

''Good.'' They talked for a few more minutes about little things, reluctant to end the call.

When she hung up, she turned to find Rita grinning at her from the doorway. ''Date tonight after all?''

Antonia smiled, afraid she might be blushing. "Yes. This is so stupid. I feel like I'm in high school."

"That's great. I wish I felt like I was in high school again. I remember when Roberto used to call me on the phone...." She heaved a dramatic sigh, closing her eyes blissfully. "We would sit there on the phone for hours until my papa chased me off. We didn't have anything to say half the time, but we couldn't bear to stop talking to each other."

"Yeah. But you'd think that by thirty, I would be past that."

"Don't be silly. Why would you want to be past that? That's what's fun. I mean, don't get me wrong. Having four kids together and knowing he's always there at home, waiting for you, knowing you can count on him—that's great. That's what life is made of. But there's nothing like that just-falling-in-love feeling."

"Falling in love?" Antonia looked at her, startled, her stomach clenching. "We are not falling in love. I like Daniel, but that's all."

Rita shot her friend a get-real look. "Sure. That's what I'm seeing, that I-light-up-like-a-Christmas-tree-when-he-calls-me-but-we're-really-just-friends look."

"I'm not saying we're just friends," Antonia protested, sure now that she was blushing. "But I am not falling in love with him. I scarcely know him. I mean, we aren't kids. We've each been through one marriage already. We aren't going to tumble head-over-heels in love."

"Uh-huh. Have you looked in the mirror lately? I think your nose is growing."

"Rita! It's the truth."

"Whatever you say. I'm not going to argue with you. But let me tell you, *chica,* you are talking to the Queen of Romance here, and I know tumbling head-over-heels when I see it."

Antonia grimaced. Rita loved to dramatize things; it was true that she was the Queen of Romance. There was nothing she liked more than a love story. *She was doubtless just making the whole thing into something bigger than it was, simply because that was what she wanted it to be.*

This whole thing with Daniel was delightful, of course. Antonia couldn't deny that. It did make her smile just to hear his voice on the phone, and she couldn't help feeling excited at the thought of seeing him again this evening. *But that was not the same thing as love!* This was just a transitory feeling, delightful while it lasted, but soon gone. It wasn't love. She would never fall into that trap again.

Antonia took special care with her appearance, wishing that she had enough time to go to a store and buy a new dress. Rita, however, assured her that only a trip into San Antonio, a good hour away, would provide the sort of dress she would want, so Antonia settled for conducting a major search through her wardrobe. With the help of her friend, who had an unerring eye for color and style, she was able to pull together a look that was at the same time eye-catching yet low-key enough for a night out in Hammond. It was, Rita indicated with much head shaking and cluckings of her tongue, a monumental task, given the bland practicality of Antonia's wardrobe.

"Don't you own anything that isn't a neutral tone?" she asked at one point, exasperated by the beiges, tans and muted greens that kept turning up on Antonia's hangers. "I am *so* going to have to take you on a shopping expedition."

Finally, however, Rita managed to find a soft pink blouse with a draped neckline that she deemed suitably romantic, which she teamed with a beige skirt that was shorter than most of the ones Antonia owned, and strappy sandals that would add, she promised, exactly the right touch of sexual allure. Looking in the mirror, Antonia had to admit that Rita was right, clear down to the lustrous touch of pearl earrings.

They had followed the green mask with several other esoteric lotions and toners that Rita assured Antonia were vital to her skin. Then they had done a complete manicure and pedicure. Antonia had followed all that up with a long soak in an herbal bath solution before she dressed and put on her makeup.

The look on Daniel's face when he arrived at her doorstep later that evening confirmed that the afternoon's efforts had been worth it. He pulled her to him for a long kiss, and for a moment Antonia seriously considered opting for another evening at home.

They went to an Italian restaurant in Hammond, the nearest town of any size. In truth, the Moonstone's food was probably better than anything that Hammond had to offer, but Hammond had the advantage of their being able to eat together without being under public scrutiny. Afterward, they went to a movie, one that, as Daniel had predicted, had already played in Houston while Antonia was still living there. It was, in short, a pleasant, but mundane evening—except that nothing about it felt mundane in the slightest.

The whole evening was infused with the remembrance of the night they had spent together. Antonia could not look at Daniel without thinking of his kisses, of the way his callused hands had drifted over her. Her body hummed with a low, intense sexual awareness even as they spoke of trivialities or laughed over a shared story. When they walked from the car to the restaurant, he took her hand, and that mere touch made her grow warm all over. Sitting beside him in the movie, she could barely keep her mind on the plot, so aware was she of Daniel's heat beside her, of the brush of his arm against hers. Everything seemed brighter, funnier, more dazzling, filled with anticipation.

They both knew what would happen when the movie was over and they drove back home. With each moment that passed, their anticipation grew. Daniel's hand covered hers on the seat between them, and she could feel the almost imperceptible warming of his skin as they grew closer and closer to Angel Eye. They were silent; Antonia could think of nothing to say. Her head was filled with jumbled, heated images of Daniel's body pressed against hers. His foot grew leaden on the accelerator; they zoomed through the night.

They reached the outskirts of Angel Eye. A few blocks, one red light, and they would be to Antonia's house. Her breath came a little faster in her throat. She shifted in her seat.

At that moment there was a flash of red-and-blue lights behind them, and the short whine of a siren turned on and immediately turned off again as a car pulled onto the road behind them.

Daniel let out a groan and a soft curse, and came to a stop on the shoulder of the road.

Chapter 9

"Cops?" Antonia asked, craning her head around to see behind them. "Oh, no..." Her regret was as much for the jarring interruption to her plans as for the possibility of a traffic ticket.

Daniel blew out a long sigh of disgust. "Oh, yes...and I think I know just which one."

Antonia glanced at him, wondering what he meant, just as a tall, well-built man in a tan sheriff's uniform strolled up to the window. Daniel touched the window button and rolled it down. The law officer peered into the window, his face expressionless.

"You know how fast you were going, sir?" he asked sternly.

Daniel favored him with a lethal look. "No. Why don't you tell me?"

Antonia glanced at Daniel, startled by his surly attitude.

"Well, let's just say it was well over the speed limit. In a hurry to get home, huh?" His mouth twitched slightly, and his brown eyes danced. "I'm afraid I'm going to have to ask you folks to step out of the car." He looked across at Antonia. "You, too, ma'am."

Antonia stared at him in astonishment for a moment before all the pieces fell into place. This was Daniel's brother, the county sheriff.

"For Pete's sake, Quinn, couldn't you be a little less dramatic?" Daniel grumbled, opening the door and stepping out.

Antonia slid across the seat and got out after him, looking at the sheriff with interest. He swept off his hat and nodded to her, unable to keep a grin from breaking across his face. In the glow of the streetlight, Antonia could see that there was some resemblance to Daniel in the shape of his face and mouth, though the difference in their coloring was enough that she would probably not have recognized him as Daniel's brother immediately. His eyes were a lighter brown than Daniel's, and his hair was a dark auburn, with the lighter brows and skin that usually accompanied the shade of his hair. Individually, she could see that many of their features were similar, but there was a spark of mischief in his eyes and a dimple in his grin that gave him a certain impish quality.

"Hello, ma'am." Quinn smiled at her. "Sorry if I alarmed you. But some people you simply have to pull over to get their attention." He glanced back at Daniel, his eyebrows going up in a devilish way.

"You didn't have to turn on the lights," Daniel

griped, even though he smiled back at his brother. "I told you I would introduce you to her."

"You're too slow," Quinn retorted. "I decided I had to take matters into my own hands." He turned back to Antonia. "Quinn Sutton, ma'am, sheriff of Burton County. And, I'm forced to admit, brother of this guy here. Frankly," he went on in a confidential tone, his eyes twinkling, "I was afraid that fact might cost me the election."

"Yeah, right," Daniel stuck in sardonically.

"I'm Antonia Campbell," Antonia replied, smiling back at him and extending her hand. "Pleased to meet you, Sheriff Sutton."

"Quinn, ma'am, please. Otherwise I'll think I've offended you, and I *would* be sorry for that."

"Quinn, then," Antonia agreed, shaking his hand. "Perhaps you'd like to come back to the house with us for a cup of coffee. I might even be able to find some dessert."

"I'm sure he can't," Daniel began.

"That sounds real nice," Quinn said at the same time, glancing over at his brother with a grin.

"I thought you were on duty?" Daniel said pointedly.

"No, I'm off. Just happened to be out when I saw you. You know, my nightly drive down Mrs. Ramirez's street. Coffee sounds great. Give us a chance to talk."

"Mmm," Daniel agreed a trifle sourly.

So the three of them got back in their vehicles and drove to Antonia's.

"That kid always had a knack of getting in my way," Daniel grumbled as he started the pickup.

Antonia chuckled. "Don't be grumpy. I think it'll be fun to get to know your brother."

"It wasn't exactly what I had in mind for the evening." He cast a look at Antonia that left her in little doubt as to what Daniel had planned.

Heat stirred in her abdomen. "Well..." she pointed out, "Quinn won't be there the rest of the night."

"That's true." Daniel smiled. "And I've always been able to outwait him."

She made a pot of coffee when they got to her house and rummaged around in her freezer until she found a small frozen cake at the back. Not exactly gourmet fare, she reflected, but, then, Daniel might as well find out early that her skills didn't lie in the kitchen.

They lounged around the living room, talking and sipping coffee. Antonia found she liked Quinn although he was very different from Daniel, possessing a sort of mischievous Texas-style charm that was hard to resist. He told tales about their boyhood that Antonia was not sure were entirely factual but were definitely entertaining. It was a little hard, she thought, to picture him as a law enforcement officer.

But when Daniel jokingly brought up the subject of his drives down Mrs. Ramirez's street, Quinn was suddenly all business. He straightened, humor dropping from his face, and the warm brown eyes were suddenly sharp and intense. At that moment, she had no trouble believing that he was the sheriff.

"There's something going on there," Quinn said.

"What?" Daniel's brows rose. "You're joking. They're dealing drugs on Jefferson Street?"

Quinn shrugged. "I'm not sure what it is. But there's a suspicious amount of activity. There are lots of cars. People coming and going. It's odd. It's always been a nice, respectable neighborhood, and the house belongs to some old man I've never heard anything bad about. That's what got Mrs. Ramirez in such a twitter. So I put Ruben Padilla on it. They all know he's a deputy, of course, but he can still get more information than I can."

The grin flashed again, and Quinn settled back in his chair, the sheriff persona retreating behind a pleasant mask. "Enough of that kind of talk. I reckon I'd better get moving." He shot a laughing glance at Daniel. "Though I know you hate for me to leave."

"Oh, yeah," Daniel replied dryly. "I'd been hoping the three of us would hang out a couple of hours, at least." He grinned. "But maybe I can return the favor sometime."

Quinn let out a short bark of laughter. "Now, Dan, let's not get testy." He rose, picking up his hat and going over to Antonia. "It was a pleasure meeting you. And if you should ever come to your senses about this guy..." He jerked a thumb back toward his brother and grinned. "You know where to find me."

"Thanks, I'll keep that in mind," Antonia said with a wry smile as Daniel snorted in the background.

Daniel walked his brother to the door, then turned and came back to Antonia.

"I liked your brother," Antonia told him.

"Women always seem to," Daniel said, shaking his head at the mystery of it.

"But..." she went on, linking her hands behind Daniel's neck and looking up at him with a sensual smile "...all I can say is, 'Thank God he's gone.'"

Daniel let out a chuckle and wrapped his arms around her, lifting her up into him as his lips came down to meet hers.

Antonia would not have said she was unhappy before she met Daniel Sutton; if anyone had asked, she would have replied that she was pleased with her job and content in her life, not wanting any more. Yet now, since she had started seeing Daniel, it was as if a switch had been turned on. Suddenly everything seemed brighter—the colors deeper, the jokes funnier, the people nicer, the problems easier. Somehow all the bumps just evened out, and every morning when she woke up, she found herself looking forward to the day ahead.

She put the odd phone calls to a stop. She realized that she had been foolish in not doing something earlier—*why had she just let it drag on?* She called the telephone company and changed her number to an unlisted one, then arranged with the clinic to have her emergency calls routed through a beeper, explaining that she had been getting harassing phone calls. It had been easily done, and no one at the clinic had thought it was at all odd. She wondered why she had thought she would have to tell everyone about Alan if she admitted to the phone calls. It had been the old paralyzing fear at work, she realized, the inertia that had always swamped her in the face of Alan's brutality, dragging her under.

Talking about it to Daniel had allowed her to free herself of that weight. It wasn't that he had done anything. It was just...easier. Somehow, everything with Daniel was easier.

Scarcely even noticing that it was happening, Antonia found herself seeing Daniel more and more as spring turned into summer. She saw him every weekend, and they would often get together during the week, as well. They went to movies or out to eat and sometimes dancing. Other times they just stayed at home, having dinner and perhaps watching a video at Daniel's house or hers. She went with him to James's graduation, and it warmed her inside to share this moment in Daniel's and James's life.

A few times they double-dated with Quinn and whatever young woman he favored at the moment. It was never the same one twice, and Antonia wondered how he managed to maintain such a large collection of dating partners in a town the size of Angel Eye.

"Quinn doesn't limit himself to Angel Eye," Daniel assured her when she commented on it. "Lots of them are from Hammond, and there are a couple from Boerne and Bandera, places like that. He has a couple of women he sees on and off in San Antonio, too."

"Doesn't it get confusing?"

"It would to me, but apparently not to Quinn."

"He's never been serious about anyone?"

Daniel shrugged. "I'm not sure. Something happened to him when he was living in San Antonio. He was on the police force there for a few years after he got out of school. I don't know if it was a girl or police business or what, but he came back to Angel Eye, said he was tired of being a big city cop. And he's been a little different since then.''

''How?''

Daniel shrugged. ''It's hard to say. He's still full of himself and talking up a storm, but—well, there's something a little heavier about him, darker. He's not quite as lighthearted as he used to be. He always had women running after him, but it seems like he used to have more relationships than he does now—ones that lasted longer than a few dates.''

''What do you think happened to him?''

''I don't know. Could be about anything, I guess. He never talked about it.''

''Have you ever asked?''

Daniel glanced at Antonia, a little surprised. ''No. If he wants to talk about it, he will. Oh, probably our sister wormed it out of him. But I figure there are some things you can't bear to talk about.''

You mean like you and Lurleen, Antonia thought, but did not say the words aloud. Daniel hadn't mentioned his first wife since the time they had talked on the rocky bluff after James's prom. It struck her as odd that he didn't talk about her. Most people, she had found, mentioned their ex-spouses far more than one wanted to hear about them, usually in the form of complaints. The fact that Daniel did not made Antonia wonder if it was a wound that was still sore to the touch, especially given the pain she had heard in his voice that night. She was afraid that he still loved Lurleen, loved her in a deep and abiding way that could never be eradicated. *Why else would he keep pictures of her in his house? Why else had he never remarried?*

Antonia was intensely curious about the woman. She wanted to know if Daniel still loved her. But she couldn't bring herself to ask him about Lurleen outright—especially not whether he was still in love with his ex-wife. She wasn't sure she wanted to hear the answer, anyway.

Antonia didn't know why it bothered her to think that Daniel was still in love with his former wife. After all, she didn't love him, didn't expect him to love her. They had exactly the sort of relationship she wanted, friendly, comfortable, yet filled with a sexual fire that made it more exciting than any relationship she had ever had. She didn't want it to be different; she didn't want more. She didn't want Daniel to be madly in love with her or wanting to get married any more than she wanted to be madly in love with him. This happiness, this fun that had filled her life since he came into it, was more than enough. Still, she could not help but feel a twitch of unease whenever she thought of Lurleen.

"Say—" Daniel went on "—speaking of my family... Next week it's Fourth of July, and everybody's getting together out at Dad's. Beth is coming in for the week with her husband and baby, and Cater'll be down from Austin. Cory's already here. So the whole family will be there. You game to go?"

"Sure." Antonia smiled. "I'd like to meet your family."

"You better reserve judgment on that until you meet them." Daniel warned.

* * *

He was still warning her about them the next Wednesday as they drove out to his father's ranch. "Now, don't let 'em overwhelm you. They can be a bit much to take sometimes."

"I'll be okay," Antonia assured Daniel, casting him an amused glance. He had been antsy from the moment he picked her up at her house.

"Well, Cory can talk you to death. And if Beth and Quinn tag team you..."

A giggle burst from Antonia's throat. "Honestly, Daniel, you make your family sound like they're going to trap me and badger me into something."

"Oh, they wouldn't upset you for the world!" Daniel assured her, looking even more worried. "Ah, I've made it worse. Now you'll be looking for them to bother you. They're really very nice. It's just...there are several of them, and they all have this...this thing about me."

"This thing?" Antonia looked at him askance. "What thing?"

"Oh, they think I'm lonely and...oh, you know. They're always trying to fix me up with somebody."

"So are you afraid that they're going to try to convince me to marry you, or that they'll think I'm not worthy of you?"

"They would never think that!" Daniel looked faintly shocked. "They're not stupid. They know you're all class."

Antonia smiled. "Why, thank you. I'll remember that next time I'm elbow deep in horse intestines."

"I'm afraid they'll be trying to sell you on me, telling you what a great guy I am, what a wonderful father I've been. Nudging, poking, hinting..." He looked pained. "Cory and Quinn can talk the paint off the wall. And Beth's the worst, now that she's married and has the baby. She's positive that what everybody needs is to get married, then they'll be perfectly happy."

"Ah..." Antonia said, nodding wisely. "Now I see. You're afraid that your sister and I will get together and cook up a scheme to trap you into marriage."

"No! I mean, you'd never—I know you don't want to trap me into marrying you." He cast her a horrified look. "I'm not saying anything about you. I'm afraid that they will scare you away with all their—" he made a vague gesture, fumbling for the right word "—their talking!"

Antonia had to chuckle. She leaned over and patted Daniel's hand on the wheel. "I have to tell you, talking doesn't scare me nearly as much as it does you."

Daniel smiled weakly. "You think I'm nuts, don't you?"

"No. I think you're nervous about my meeting your family, and that's kind of sweet. But I'm sure I'll like them all. And if I should get to feeling like I need to run away, I'll come and tell you that I want to leave. I promise I won't assume that whatever they tell me, they're speaking for you."

"Really?" Daniel looked relieved.

"Really."

Antonia could understand why the quiet and reserved Daniel felt somewhat anxious about his family, for as soon as he pulled to a stop in front of his father's house, the front door was flung open and a tall woman with wildly curling red hair came flying out.

"Daniel!" she shrieked and ran down the steps and across the yard toward Daniel's truck. She launched herself at him from several feet away, throwing her arms around his neck and hugging him fiercely. "Lord, it's so good to see you again! What took you so long? James got here ages ago. Why won't you ever come out to L.A. to visit me?"

"Aw, Beth..." Daniel returned her hug. "You know I wouldn't last two minutes in a place like that."

"I know, I know." From her tone of voice, this was obviously a topic that had been discussed many times in the past. "You're just a country boy."

Beth stepped back, gave her brother a long, searching look, then turned to Antonia. "You must be Antonia. Quinn's told me all about you." She held out her hand. "You're just as beautiful as he said. I thought he was exaggerating. Quinn's prone to do that. But this time he was right on the mark."

"Thank you." Antonia gave her a slightly embarrassed smile.

"Now, don't talk her to death, Beth," Daniel said warningly.

"Honestly, Daniel...you would think I was still ten years old, the way you talk." She paused, then admitted, "Actually, I have been kind of a chatterbox today, but it's so good to be home. L.A. is just so—so—not Texas."

"I don't know how you stand it," Daniel commented. "Or how you even breathe, come to that."

"Hey, listen, Houston has as many ozone days as

L.A. now,'' Beth pointed out as she turned and walked with them toward the front door. ''It's not that, anyway. But the people are different and, well, when you're married to Jackson Prescott, it's hard to be ordinary folks. Lots of times it's fun—going to movie premieres and all that. But sometimes, like when some paparazzi takes pictures of you at the grocery store, it's too much.''

As they reached the front door, it opened, and a very tall young man stepped out, holding a toddler in one arm. The baby immediately began to bounce up and down and grin, holding out his arms to his mother.

''Hey, honey,'' Beth said, taking the child, who then instantly turned back around and held out his hands to the young man again.

The man grinned. ''Wanna come back, big fella?'' He reached out and took the toddler, settling him with practiced ease into the crook of his arm again. ''Hey, Daniel. Good to see you.''

''Cory. How you doing? How's Austin?''

''Same as ever.''

Cory was taller than his oldest brother by at least two or three inches and looked closer in age to James, Daniel's son, than to Daniel. From what Daniel had told her about him, Antonia knew that he was a junior at the University of Texas, but his boyish good looks made him appear even younger than his twenty-one years. His eyes were large and lighter than Daniel's—green or blue, Antonia couldn't quite tell—and his unruly brown hair was several shades lighter, as well. His wide, mobile mouth, now stretched into a wide grin, and the pale dusting of freckles across his cheeks contributed to the youthfulness of his face—as did the small bump that ruined the straight line of his nose.

Cory turned his wide, inquisitive gaze on Antonia, and his grin grew broader. "Hi. I'm Cory."

"Antonia Campbell."

"Quinn tells me you're a vet," Cory said. "That's cool. I'd have been better about taking Moonshine to the vet's if you'd been there, wouldn't I, Beth?"

"No doubt," Beth retorted dryly. "But I'm not sure that such rampant sexism is anything to brag about, Cory."

"Aw, Beth, that's not sexism." He looked a little uncertainly at Antonia. "Is it?"

Antonia had to smile. "I don't know. I'm afraid I'm not an expert."

"Yeah, well, neither's Beth. She just likes to give me a hard time. Which I must say—" he turned to his sister, putting on an aggrieved face "—seems awful harsh to me, given the fact that I've been baby-sitting your kid all morning." He leaned his head down to the baby's, putting forehead to forehead in way that made the little boy cackle with glee. "Isn't that right, Joey? Aren't I the best nanny you've ever had?"

He nodded his head exaggeratedly, and Joey moved his head with him, giggling with the unrestrained enthusiasm that made a child's laughter so infectious.

"Coy!" The little boy cried happily and dug in his heels, arching his back and holding his arms up. "Coy! Fly!"

"Again? Don't you ever get tired? All right."

"Remember the ceiling," Beth warned, as he went

back into the house and lifted the baby up over his head.

"Yes, Mother," Cory replied, tossing the ecstatic child up into the air a few easy inches.

Antonia assumed that the warning was more automatic than anything else, for Beth casually turned back to Antonia as they walked in the door, not even looking over at her youngest brother and her child.

"Could I get you something to drink to help you face this crowd?" Beth asked good-naturedly. "Beer? Cola? There's a pitcher of lemonade in the fridge. Cater's going to make margaritas later."

There seemed to be a large number of people in the house as they strolled through the foyer and into the large family room. Daniel had a father and four siblings, and only Beth was married, as far as Antonia knew. But there were a great many more people than that milling about between the family room and kitchen, and another group on the back patio, where a black, barrel-shaped barbecue smoked and children splashed noisily in the pool. Several older, weathered men in cowboy hats, one of them Daniel's father, Marshall, were gathered around the barbecue, arms folded, talking in a desultory way. Quinn, whom Antonia recognized by his distinctive red hair, was also by the pool, wearing shorts and flip-flops and looking nothing like a sheriff. He was engaged at the moment in throwing a squirming, shrieking child into the pool. This apparently was what the young boy wanted, for he was out of the pool in a flash and running to Quinn again, arms up. A curly-haired blond girl, a trifle younger than the boy and looking very much like his sister, hung back, watching the pair with great interest.

''You wondering who everybody is?'' Beth asked astutely. She turned a sharp eye on her brother. ''Daniel, did you tell her it was just family?''

''No!'' Daniel protested, raising his hands as if in surrender. ''I didn't say that.'' He glanced a little uncertainly at Antonia. ''Did I?''

''No. I guess you didn't. I just assumed it, I suppose.''

''Well, it's mostly family,'' Daniel assured her. ''Aunts and uncles and cousins and stuff.'' He looked out the windows across the back of the house toward the pool. ''Who are those kids? Are they related to us?''

Beth giggled. ''No. They're Melanie Hanson's kids. She's in Santa Fe this summer, and she flew down to spend the Fourth with us.''

Antonia's eyes widened. ''Melanie Hanson the actress?''

Beth nodded. ''Yeah. Kind of weird, huh? I've gotten used to it, after a fashion—knowing famous people, I mean. But sometimes it still seems bizarre. Melanie's been a friend of Jackson's for years. That's Jackson over there at the table under the umbrella, reading a script.'' She shook her head in amazement. ''The man's got remarkable concentration.''

'''Course, Billy Conrad's here, too,'' Daniel put in. ''Cory's friend.''

''Yeah, and James's crew will doubtless stop by later. Benny and Dolan and that lot,'' Beth added.

Daniel turned a rueful look at Antonia. "I'm sorry. I didn't think...lots of the friends are like family."

Antonia chuckled. "Don't worry. I'm not exactly a stranger now, you know. I was at Dolan Caulfield's place last week, and he showed me the calf he's raising for his FFA project next fall."

"Did he? And is it the wonder that he claims?" Daniel asked, interested.

"Very nice. I wouldn't be surprised if he wins district with her, as long as he does what he needs to."

"Oh, Dolan will," Daniel said with the voice of long acquaintance. "That boy's so steady he's downright tiresome sometimes. Every time I think James is a slacker, I just take a look at Dolan and thank my lucky stars."

"You're thanking them for Dolan Caulfield?" a male voice inquired incredulously behind them, and they turned to see a tall, black-haired, blue-eyed man who Antonia knew immediately had to be a brother of Daniel's.

The thick black hair was much the same as Daniel's, as were the outcropping cheekbones and the lean, wide-shouldered build, so much so that even the sophisticated clothes, expertly cut hair and vivid blue eyes could not disguise the relationship between the two of them.

"Last time I was around that boy, I was just thankful to get away with only one long description of last year's Future Farmers of America project," the man continued wryly.

"Oh, yeah. The sheep." Daniel shook his head. "Dolan gets some odd notions."

"Cater!" Beth cried, stepping forward to loop her arm through his. "Oh, who cares about Dolan and his FFA stuff? Come here and meet Daniel's—ah, the new veterinarian."

Cater's eyebrows rose lazily. "Oh, yes...Daniel's new vet. I've heard a great deal about you."

He was, Antonia thought, the most decidedly handsome of the lot—and all the Sutton men were good-looking, from Cory's boyish features to Quinn's impish charm. Cater looked as if he had just stepped out of the pages of a men's fashion magazine—all designer clothes and chiseled looks—but with just enough casual imperfection to make him thoroughly masculine. Still, Antonia thought as she extended her hand to Cater to shake, she preferred Daniel's weathered face and work-muscled body to any of them, even this one.

"And I've heard a great deal about you," Antonia countered. "You're the writer, aren't you?"

"You got me there," Cater agreed amiably. "I'm the one who doesn't have a real job, as Quinn puts it."

It was easy being with Daniel's family, Antonia found. She had already discovered that about Quinn, whose banter was hard to resist. Now, as the day wore on, she realized that all of them had a way of making her feel as if she had just stepped into her own home. Quinn's way, of course, was to casually flirt with her, casting Daniel a teasing look as he did so. Cory, on the other hand, let her play with the baby, all the while relating with boyish enthusiasm his decision to change his major at the university to elementary education.

Beth eased her path through myriad friends and relatives, joining her whenever she saw that Daniel was not at Antonia's side. And Cater had turned on what Antonia presumed was a low-wattage, brother's-girlfriend-appropriate charm and regaled her with funny stories from his most recent book-signing tour.

At first Cater's elegance made her a trifle uneasy, reminding her of the sleek, sophisticated men of Alan's and her parents' circle—until, that is, that afternoon, when he got into a wrestling match with Cory and pitched them both, fully clothed, into the pool. Quinn, standing beside the pool, had guffawed at the sight of the two of them, and they had proceeded to reach up in unison and drag him into the pool with them. All of them had come up laughing.

Antonia was sitting beneath the shade of one of the umbrellas at the time, talking to Beth, who held the baby, Joseph, sound asleep amidst the noise of the poolside. Beth, watching her brothers, rolled her eyes.

"A bunch of man-sized kids," she said with affectionate scorn. "Honestly, sometimes I wonder if men ever grow up. Or, at least, my brothers. Jackson loves hanging out with them. He says it keeps him from getting too Hollywood. I guess it does. Last Christmas when we were here, they took him to this cowboy bar over in Hammond, and he came home with a black eye. Somebody made a derogatory comment about Jackson's Italian slacks, so Quinn punched him, and then Jackson got into it, too. Daniel and Cater had to pull them out of there before they got into real trouble. Not that Cater hasn't regularly gotten into fights, too."

"Cater?" Antonia repeated. "He doesn't seem the type."

"I know—too pretty, right? That was always the bane of his existence, his looking like a model or something. That's why he used to get into fights. He doesn't have the temper Quinn does, but guys were always challenging him, and he had to show them that he wasn't just a pretty boy or a grind—he was always the best in school, especially English. In Angel Eye, being able to write poetry or an essay was not a sought-after skill. Plus, he and Quinn used to tussle regularly, being in the middle the way they are."

"It must have been quite an experience, growing up with four brothers," Antonia said.

"That's one way to put it. I learned to stand up for myself, that's for sure. On the other hand, sometimes I felt like I was going to smother, with all of them 'looking after me.'"

"I can imagine." Antonia suspected that struggling against four brothers' overprotectiveness probably had some similarities to her own struggles with her parents' plans for her life.

They were silent for a moment, and Antonia could feel Beth's speculative gaze on her. Finally Beth said in a seemingly casual tone, "Daniel seems really happy."

Antonia's gaze went again to Daniel. Arms crossed, he was listening to his uncle. Then a smile broke across his serious face, lighting it up. Antonia could not keep from smiling herself, watching him.

"Yeah. He likes his life, I think."

"Mmm," Beth murmured noncommittally. After a

while she started again. ''But I think he's happier now.''

Antonia turned to look at her. She couldn't deny the little spurt of joy she felt inside at the implication of Beth's words. ''Really?''

Beth nodded. ''He—well, Daniel doesn't show much of his feelings. You know, he's got that old stoic cowboy thing he has to keep up. Gets that from Dad. But his first marriage was tough.''

The familiar curiosity about Lurleen stirred in Antonia. ''I know it must have been hard raising a child all by himself,'' she said carefully. ''But I don't know much about his first marriage.''

Beth's face tightened. ''Well, you won't hear anything good about Lurleen from me—or anyone else who loves Daniel. She made him miserable.''

Antonia's heart squeezed painfully in her chest—although she wasn't sure how much of the pain was from the thought of Daniel being hurt and how much came from the idea that he had loved another woman so much that she had been able to hurt him that badly.

''He must have loved her very much,'' she said in a soft voice, unable to meet Beth's eyes.

Beth's eyes flashed with long-held resentment. ''Yeah. He did that. You would have thought the sun rose and set in Lurleen. Personally, I never liked her.'' She sighed and added honestly, '''Course I wouldn't have liked anybody who took Daniel away from our family. I was just a kid when he married her, and I adored Daniel. But we could all see that he wasn't happy. At least, he wasn't happy for long.''

"Daniel said she didn't like living in a small town," Antonia prodded when Beth said nothing more.

"She didn't like marriage either," Beth added bitterly. "Oh, maybe I'm too hard on her. I mean, I wanted to get away from Angel Eye, too. I felt like I was imprisoned here—everybody knowing everything about me, my brothers and father always keeping their eye on me. And she was way too young to be married and have a kid—they had James only a year after they got married. But why did she marry him if that was the way she felt? Everybody knew that Daniel loved it here, that this was all he wanted to do with his life. She couldn't have been that stupid. If she wanted to see the world, why didn't she go off and see it right after high school instead of marrying Daniel? It would have hurt him, but surely not as much as it did when she was married to him and left him with a little boy to raise."

"People don't act reasonably when they're young and in love." Antonia thought about her own marriage and her foolish blindness to the signs of Alan's true nature.

"I know. But I can't help but think Lurleen was wickedly selfish. She wanted Daniel, and she thought she could change him, make him move to San Antonio or someplace after they were married. Lurleen always figured she was entitled to have everything her way." She smiled wryly. "I'm sorry. I sound horribly bitter, don't I? I can't help it, though. She made Daniel so unhappy. That's what I remember about him from those years—that he was sad all the time, first fighting with Lurleen, then missing her when she was gone, trying to do his best by James and not let him see how sad and miserable he was. He was crazy about her. I don't know if he ever got over it, really.''

Beth, caught up in her own memories, wasn't looking at Antonia and didn't see the flicker of pain that crossed Antonia's face at her words. Antonia herself was a little surprised at how much it hurt to hear of Daniel's love for another woman. It was, after all, what she had already suspected. Yet, like a tongue seeking out a sore tooth, she could not help but explore the idea.

''He's loved her all these years?''

Beth nodded. ''He's a faithful kind of guy. I don't think it's an open wound or anything anymore. He's dated some, and he's content—there's James and his horses, and he loves that life. But Lurleen wasn't really out of his life. You know? He carried a torch for her for years. He didn't get a divorce, even though she had left him. They stay married for several years after she left, and then it was Lurleen who sued for divorce. I know she called him several times needing money, and he always sent it to her. Once, about four years ago, she came back to town, and she stayed with them for a couple of weeks. We were all afraid they were going to get back together.''

Pain sliced through Antonia. Daniel had not told her any of these things. He had told her about Lurleen's leaving, but he had not mentioned that the process had dragged on for years, with his ex-wife coming back to him for money and even a temporary reconciliation. Indeed, he had made it sound as if it had all been over long, long ago. *Why had he not told her all this?* Antonia could think of only one reason—it was a subject that was still too painful to him, too close to his heart.

Beth smiled at Antonia. "You can see why we're all so happy that he's found you."

"I understand," Antonia replied, relieved to find that she could keep her voice even and dispassionate, despite the clutch of pain in her chest. "You want him to be in love with somebody else instead of Lurleen."

"We want him to be happy," Beth corrected. She frowned a little, looking down at the top of her baby's head. Slowly, as if choosing her words with care, she went on. "I would hate for Daniel to be in love with someone who didn't love him back."

"I don't think you need to worry about that," Antonia replied. *Daniel didn't love her.* It was clear to Antonia that he still carried a torch for his ex-wife.

"Good." Beth grinned.

Antonia knew that Beth had misunderstood her words, thinking that Antonia meant she reciprocated Daniel's feelings for her. *But what did it matter? Daniel did not love her, and, of course, she didn't love him, either. So why did she want to go off in a corner by herself and cry?*

It was then that she realized it, with breathtaking clarity. It mattered; it mattered horribly that Daniel was still in love with his ex-wife. And the reason was because, in spite of all her intentions and her cool-headed plans, she had fallen in love with Daniel Sutton.

Chapter 10

Daniel pulled the truck into Antonia's driveway and turned off the engine. He looked over at her. "You sure have been quiet all the way home. Tired?"

Antonia, leaning back with her head against the seat, nodded. "A little."

"Did my family wear you out?"

Antonia shook her head and smiled at him. "No. They were all very nice. I liked them."

"Good."

They got out of the truck and walked up to the front door, hand in hand. Antonia unlocked the door and turned to Daniel. "You want to come in?"

"Yeah. If you're not too tired. I, uh, I wanted to talk to you about something."

His answer surprised Antonia a little, but she said nothing, just went inside. "Would you like some coffee? I have decaf."

Mitzi leaped off the back of the couch, where she had been dozing, and wound her way around their legs, meowing pitifully. Antonia bent to pet her. "Hello, sweetie, I'm sorry. Have you been lonely? I left food for you. Did you eat it?"

Antonia went to the kitchen, Mitzi twining in and out of her legs so much that Antonia was afraid she was going trip her. She set her keys and purse down on the table, then checked the cat's bowl. It was full of food. She turned a stern face to the cat. "Look at that. You haven't eaten a bite of it."

Mitzi sat down and stared up at her solemnly, tail twitching. Antonia shook her head as she picked up the tea kettle and started to fill it with water, saying, "I don't know what I'm going to do about you, Mitz."

Daniel stopped her, putting a hand on her arm. "No, wait. I gotta talk to you first. I've been thinking about this all the way home. All day, in fact. Hell, I've been thinking about it most of this week."

Antonia turned to him, puzzled. "What is it? Is something the matter?" A clutch of fear formed in her stomach. *He was about to tell her that he no longer wanted to see her.*

"No. Nothing is the matter. The thing is..." He hesitated, then went on in a rush. "Do you think you like my family well enough to join it?"

Antonia stared at him. His words were so far from what she had imagined that she was speechless.

"I'm sorry. Now I've scared the hell out of you, haven't I?"

"I—I'm not sure what you're saying."

"I'm asking you to marry me."

"Marry you?" She still could not quite take it in. "But—but—"

"It's too sudden, isn't it?" Daniel said, frowning. "I'm not good at things like this. I know we've only been dating two or three months, but—" He shrugged. "It didn't take me long to realize that you're the woman I want to marry."

"But how can you? I mean—I can't—you still love Lurleen. I can't—I don't want to marry a man who's still in love with his first wife."

Now it was Daniel who stared at Antonia. "What?"

"You heard me. Lurleen was your—your true love. We get along well, and the sex is great, but you don't love me like you loved her."

"I should hope I don't! Half the time I wanted to strangle Lurleen. I'm not in love with her. Where did you get that idea? Good Lord, we've been divorced for years and years."

"I know that. But everybody says you're still carrying a torch for her."

"Everybody? Who is 'everybody'?"

"Well, Rita, for one." At his grimace, she went on quickly. "Your sister, for another. Just today."

"Beth?" His eyebrows shot up. "Beth told you I still loved Lurleen?" He began to curse colorfully. "My own sister! Stabbed in the back by my own sister! I'll be damned. I knew I should never have taken you to that party. Wait'll I get hold of her—"

"No, don't be mad at her. It wasn't as if she was warning me off or anything. I was the one who asked about Lurleen."

"And what did she say?"

"Well, she said that she hated Lurleen."

"That's true."

"Because Lurleen had made your life miserable."

"Yeah, we both did a pretty good job of that to each other."

"She said that you had never gotten over her, that even though Lurleen left you, you didn't file for divorce. She said that Lurleen was the one who filed several years later. And she said that Lurleen came back a few years ago and wanted to get back together, and that you all tried it for a while. That you lived together for a few weeks or something and then she left again."

"Well, Beth's just a fountain of information, isn't she?" Daniel made a disgusted face.

"It only confirmed what Rita and others have said," Antonia told him sadly. "What I've seen for myself. I mean, she left you fifteen years ago, and you've never remarried. That says something."

"It says that I never found another woman I wanted to marry until now," Daniel retorted. "That doesn't necessarily mean I'm still hung up on Lurleen. That woman and I nearly drove each other crazy. By the time she left, I was downright glad in some ways. I won't pretend it didn't break my heart. It did. And it was tough having to raise James all on my own. But even at the time, I knew it was for the best. I knew she and I would never be able to work it out. We were too different. We didn't want the same things. We didn't like the same stuff. Opposites attract sometimes, I guess, but that doesn't mean they're able to live with each other."

Antonia looked at him doubtfully. "Then why didn't you file for divorce? Why did you try to reconcile?"

"I didn't. Lurleen did come here, and she talked about getting back together, but even she knew that it was just talk. I didn't have any intention of marrying her again. We didn't live together, not like you mean it. I let her stay at the house a while. She didn't have anywhere else to go, and I felt sorry for her. And she *is* James's mother. That's all. As for not filing for divorce, I'm not sure why I didn't. At first, I think I was hoping she would come back, that somehow magically it would work out between us. Then...I don't know. I just let it slide. She was James's mother. I kind of hated to break the bond. I didn't want to let go of the past. And I had no intention of remarrying. I wasn't about to get into another marriage at that point. So I didn't do anything. She did it when she wanted to remarry, and I had no problem with it." He shrugged. "I can't help what people inferred from those things. They're wrong. I was not carrying a torch for Lurleen."

"But what about the pictures of her?" Antonia cried. "I've seen them in your house. You still keep pictures of her in your living room. And you never talk about her. That's a little strange."

Daniel's eyebrows shot up. "You think I still love her because I *don't* talk about her? I don't talk about her because she has nothing to do with my life. I don't mind talking about her. I just don't have anything to say. And the pictures are there because she's James's mother, even if the two of us are divorced. It wouldn't be right to pretend she didn't exist, to put away all the pictures of his mother like she was an enemy or something. Lurleen never gave two flips about the kid. He knows it. I mean, she left him without a qualm. She would come back and see him maybe once a year. There for a while, she didn't see him for three years in a row. I hate Lurleen for that. But I'm not going to reinforce the fact that she's had nothing to do with his life."

"Oh." Antonia looked at him, trying to adjust to this change.

"Look," Daniel went on, crossing to her and taking her hand in his. "I loved Lurleen, but I don't love her still. It was a teenage thing, full of drama and angst and fighting and hormones. It wasn't the way I love you. I love you because I know you. Because I want to be with you all the time. I have more fun with you than with anybody, and I can't imagine spending the rest of my life not being with you. Well, there's the hormone thing, too, but…"

"You love me?" Antonia asked a little breathlessly.

"Of course I love you!" He looked at her in astonishment. "You think I would ask you to marry me if I didn't love you?" He grinned, the corners of his eyes crinkling.

"Oh, Daniel!" Antonia threw her arms around him, holding on to him tightly. "I love you, too."

He squeezed her to him, his head against hers. Finally he released her and stepped back a little, looking down into her face. "And what about marrying me?"

Her stomach clenched in anxiety. "I—I'm not sure.

I want to—it's just—I swore I would never marry again.''

''I'm not like him, Antonia.''

''I know. I know you're not. But I—can I think about it? Just a while? I can't rush into it.''

''Sure. I understand.'' He smiled and bent to kiss her lightly on the lips. ''I'll even leave so you can think about it.''

''No. Don't go.''

He smiled. ''Well, not for a while.''

It was some time before he left. They didn't do anything except sit on the couch, holding each other, talking a little now and then. It was enough just to be together in the glow of their love.

But finally, with a sigh, Daniel rose, saying, ''I have to get back home. I've got to get up early tomorrow, take a horse to a guy in West Texas. And you've got to think.''

''I will.'' Antonia smiled and kissed him.

''I'll call you tomorrow night when I get back.''

''Okay. I'll be waiting.''

She walked him to the door, and they kissed goodbye again. Then he walked away, and she closed the door, leaning back against it, smiling dreamily. *Marriage! Who would have thought the day would turn out like this?*

She drifted over to the couch, unable to keep from smiling to herself. She hadn't been able to stop smiling for the past hour. *Daniel loved her!* She stood for a moment beside her couch, looking down at it without seeing it, her mind far away, thinking about what it would be like to be married to Daniel.

The doorbell rang. Antonia turned, smiling, thinking that Daniel had come back. She strode to the front door and pulled it open.

A man stood on her front porch, but it was not Daniel. Antonia felt as if all the wind had been knocked out of her. She froze, staring at the man who had once been her husband. He looked older and yet, strangely, so much the same that it made her shiver.

Stupid! Why had she not looked through her peep-hole before she opened the door? She had grown careless, especially since she had started seeing Daniel. She felt so good with him, so safe and secure, that she had put Alan out of her mind. She had come to expect only Daniel at the front door.

Fear licked along her nerves. It was all she could do to keep herself from turning and running away screaming. She forced herself to speak and was pleased that her voice, though tight, did not come out laced with fear.

''What are you doing here? Get out.'' She was finally able to move, and she started to push the door closed.

''No, wait. Hear me out.'' Alan put his hand up, bracing it against the door, and moved forward a step so that he stood in the doorway. He wore a pleading expression, tentative and sincere. ''Just give me a chance to explain.''

''Explain what?'' Antonia knew that she could not close the door against him; he was too strong. But she did not want to emphasize her weakness, so she decided not to struggle to close it. She assumed an aloof listening expression, the face of someone who could not be fooled, but who was fair enough to listen.

"I've changed," he began earnestly.

"I've heard that before."

"No, I really have this time. It's different. I'm different." He sidled the rest of the way into the room, letting go of the door. She could close it now, but there was no way she would, not with him inside the house with her. "I've changed. Honestly."

She cursed inwardly, hating herself for letting him work his way around her yet again. She shouldn't have answered the door without looking. *And why had she frozen like that when she saw him, letting him block the door?* Antonia despised her fear; it had always immobilized her. She had believed that she had gotten much stronger and braver the past few years—yet she had given him no resistance at all.

"I hope you have," she said, holding the door open as she faced him. "For your sake."

"For both our sakes," he responded. "Antonia, close the door. I'm not going to hurt you. Let's sit down and talk like civilized adults."

Mitzi stalked into the room and sat down a few feet away from Alan, regarding him balefully. When he paid no attention to her, Mitzi let out an imperative meow. Alan glanced at her dismissively, then turned back to Antonia. Mitzi hissed and stood up, her fur rising all over her body, until she looked like a huge puffball with a little head in front. The cat, Antonia thought, had more sense than most humans.

"I don't think that's possible, Alan. Just tell me

what you came to say and leave.'' She prayed that he did not detect the faint quiver underlying her voice. She remained by the door, one hand on the knob. She could run out the door, she thought, and maybe reach her car in the drive before he could get to her. The problem was that she did not have the keys, which were sitting beside her purse on the kitchen table.

''I talked to your mother,'' he began, moving toward the couch. The room was arranged so that the back of the couch was to the door, and Alan sat casually on the back, legs braced in front of him and his arms crossed over his chest. He was several feet away from her, and the distance gave her some sense of relief. Unfortunately, he was also between her and the kitchen, and Antonia had to have the keys in order to escape him.

Balding, dressed in his yuppie lawyer casual clothes, with a sort of unassuming handsomeness, he looked completely harmless. Antonia knew that anyone, looking at him, would have found it hard to believe that he was a wife-batterer. There was nothing violent and brutish about Alan; he was urbane, witty, polite. It had been one of the reasons why it had taken Antonia so long to realize that the beatings and his temper had not been her fault—it had been hard even for her to accept that this man could do the things he had done. However, she knew him too well now to fall for his harmless look—or for his assurance that he would not hurt her.

''I know. She told me,'' Antonia replied. She knew that she had to take action. She could not just let Alan come in and control the conversation. Even though it scared her, she closed the door and stepped away from it. "If you insist on talking, why don't we sit down and have a cup of coffee?" She tried to keep her voice irritated enough that Alan would not be suspicious, yet not so unfriendly that her offer of refreshment was unbelievable. Without waiting for an answer, she strode toward the kitchen, slanting across the floor past him. Mitzi turned and ran alongside her. It was extremely hard to walk away from him, her back exposed. There was never any telling what Alan would do.

This time, to her relief, he made no move to grab her or attack her from the back. Instead he levered away from the couch and walked after her to the kitchen. "Coffee sounds good," he said, surprise tinging his voice. "Decaf, if you have it. I'm glad you're willing to consider the idea."

Antonia walked into the kitchen ahead of him, picking up her purse and setting it aside on the counter and at the same time palming the keys. With her back to him, she stuck the keys in her front pocket as she reached up with the other hand to open the cabinet and take down a can of coffee.

"I'm not considering any idea, Alan," she told him flatly as she moved about, filling the drip coffeemaker with grounds and water. "Offering someone coffee scarcely constitutes agreement. As I told Mother, I am glad for you that you have changed." She turned around to face him, her back to the counter, crossing her arms. "But personally, it doesn't matter to me. You are not part of my life anymore."

"I understand how you feel," Alan replied reasonably. "You're hurt, angry.... I was wrong. Terribly, terribly wrong. But I've changed. It will be different this time."

"I've heard that before, Alan. But it never worked."

"I know. That was my fault." Alan spread his hands out to the sides in a gesture of culpability and regret. "I was too jealous, too crazy about you. I should have trusted you. I should have learned to control my temper. I see all that now. And I want to make it up to you."

Antonia wondered if there was any basis of truth to his words, if he really had gone to therapy and tried to make a change. Alan had always had the ability to sound so reasonable and candid that she had felt guilty and illogical for not believing what he said. However, she knew that if he really had changed, he would not have made the trip out here to try to persuade her to return to him.

"The only way you can make it up to me is by staying out of the rest of my life," Antonia replied dryly. "You keep away from me for the next forty or fifty years, and I'll call us even." She turned away, making herself busy with taking out coffee mugs and spoons, opening the refrigerator to pull out the milk jug.

Alan smiled faintly, as if she had made a joke. "Antonia..."

"Alan, it's useless. I told Mother that. She should have relayed that message to you."

"She tried to. But I know you pretty well, Antonia." He gave her an affectionate, indulgent look that sent a sizzle of annoyance up Antonia's spine. "You can talk tough, but inside you're the same sweet girl I married."

"No," Antonia said flatly. "I'm not."

"I knew if you could see me, talk to me," Alan went on as if she hadn't spoken, "if you could realize the truth of it—I want you back, Antonia. I never stopped loving you. No matter how wrongheaded I was, no matter how badly I acted, you know that I loved you. I just didn't handle it well."

"No, I don't know that you loved me," Antonia replied bluntly. "You loved to control me. You loved to have the upper hand. That's not loving a person, Alan."

The coffeemaker had stopped, and she filled the mugs, adding milk and sugar to them.

"You still know how I like my coffee," Alan remarked smugly. "You see—I know you still care."

"A good memory doesn't mean I care," she snapped, picking up her cup and walked around him back into the living room.

Alan got his coffee and followed her. Mitzi brought up the rear and took up a position several feet away from Alan, still watching him intently. He glanced at the cat, and irritation tinged his voice as he said, "What is the matter with that cat? Why does it keep staring at me?"

Antonia shrugged. "I don't know. Maybe she admires you. Mitzi's taste often leaves something to be desired."

Anger flashed across Alan's face and was gone almost before she realized it had been there. He went on in a calm tone. "I know that I was too demanding, too controlling. It's difficult for me to give up control to anyone, even you. I talked about all that with my therapist, believe me. I see the issues in my life now—the problems I had with my Dad and all. I have really worked at coming to understand myself. If you would just sit down and talk to me, give me a chance, I know you'd see that for yourself."

Antonia had walked past the couch and was close once again to the front door. Alan set his mug down on the coffee table. "Come on. Come sit with me on the couch. Let's talk."

"Alan, this is pointless."

"No! It's not." He came around the couch toward her. Antonia clenched her teeth and tightened all over to keep from moving back from him. She was determined not to let him see the fear that he engendered in her. "Don't you see, Antonia? We could make it work this time! I want you in my life again. I want a home, a family—don't you?"

"Not with you," Antonia shot back.

His eyebrows drew together, and a wave of cold washed through Antonia's stomach. She thought to herself that she should not have said what she did so bluntly; Alan would be furious. In the next instant, she hated the fact that, after all this time and work, she still responded in such a fear-based way.

"Look," she said quickly, partially turning away to set down her own coffee mug on the table behind her. "Let's not get into any ugliness. Why don't we just part now before we say hurtful things?" She looked at him earnestly, hoping, despite all her experience to the contrary, that Alan would listen to reason. "We don't belong together, Alan. If you have changed, then that's wonderful, and I think you should start another life—with someone else. We would always have the past hanging over us. It wouldn't be good for you, and I know that I can't live that way. I don't want to go back. We *can't* go back."

"I'm not talking about going back. I'm talking about a new life. The two of us. I still love you, Antonia. I want to make it up to you. I want to show you how different it can be."

Antonia crossed her arms in a defensive gesture. "I have a new life now, Alan. It's the life I want, and it's here, in this place, doing what I enjoy doing. I have no intention of moving back East, let alone being your wife again. You need to accept that, Alan, and move on."

His face darkened. "What is it about this one-horse town you like so much? That cowboy?"

Antonia stiffened. "What are you talking about?"

"You think I didn't know? Didn't see?"

"You've been spying on me?" The coldness in Antonia's midsection spread all through her.

"I saw him bring you home tonight," Alan went on, the pleading sincerity gone now, replaced by a tight, clipped tone. "I saw you come inside with him for a long time. I saw you kiss him good-night at the door. Good God, Antonia—a hayseed! Do you think he can give you the kind of life that I can? Don't you have any more respect for yourself than that? Are you trying to hurt me? Shame me?"

"Who I date has nothing to do with you," Antonia

responded, struggling to hide the quiver of fear that darted through her at the way his face and voice had changed. ‘‘It has been four years, Alan. You are not in my life anymore.’’

‘‘Don’t be a fool,’’ he snapped, his features twisting with anger. ‘‘I will always be in your life. We love each other. We always have and we always will. We were meant for each other—remember, you said that.’’

‘‘No. I don’t remember. If I said that, it was obviously when I was young and foolish. When we were first married.’’

‘‘You could feel that way again if you’d only let yourself! If you’d only try again. Why won’t you give me another chance? You’re so damned obstinate! I love you, Antonia. I have loved you all four years that you’ve been gone. I tried not to. I tried dating other people. I even lived with one or two. But it was never the same. *You* were the one I wanted. *You* are the woman I love.’’

‘‘You don’t love me. Maybe you have some kind of obsession about me. Some inability to let go and move on. That isn’t love.’’

‘‘And love is what you have with Tex there?’’ he asked sarcastically, flinging his arm out toward the door.

‘‘I don’t know! It doesn’t matter. What matters is that I don’t love you! I don’t want to come back to you. I won’t—ever. You’re wasting your time here, Alan. If you really had changed, really had worked on your problems, you wouldn’t be here now, trying to get me back. I want you to leave. Now. Before I call the police.’’

"You're threatening me?" His eyes were as cold and hard now as she remembered them, black with the icy anger that had terrified her when they were married, and his body was taut, fairly resonating with fury and resentment. "You think you have the right to tell me what to do?"

"I am not threatening you. I'm telling you that you are not welcome here, and I don't intend to keep on talking to you. Our marriage is over. I am not going back to Virginia with you or anyone else. I don't want to see you or hear from you again. I don't want to get those stupid, creepy phone calls from you anymore. I don't want you following me and spying on me. If you continue to do so, I will get another injunction against you. And this time, if you hurt me or continue to harass me, I will have you put in jail. You aren't anybody here, Alan. You don't have any influential cronies. They won't have any problem arresting you or convicting you. And I don't need that divorce any longer, so your bargaining chip is gone. You will go to jail if you do anything to me. And now our conversation is over and it's time for you to leave."

Alan's face went white, as it always did when he was furious, and his hand lashed out, gripping her upper arm so tightly that Antonia was sure she would have bruises there in the morning. He leaned forward, his eyes narrowed and cruel, his face the contorted mask of her nightmares.

"Our conversation is through when I say it's through!" he hissed. "You don't tell me what to do. You are still my wife. You will always be my wife, and if you think that running and hiding from me for four years will change that, you're dead wrong. That hick can't keep you from me.'' He jerked her arm, making her stumble.

His grip hurt her arm, but far worse was the heart-pounding fear that shot through her. Antonia would never forget that look in his eyes, that tone to his voice; it chilled her to the bone.

''Do you understand me?'' he barked, shaking her.

Antonia's hand went blindly behind her and fastened on the coffee mug. Quickly she swung it out and up, sending the hot contents full into Alan's face, followed by the cup crashing painfully into his cheekbone.

Alan howled and jumped back, his hand flying to his face. Antonia whirled and darted out the front door.

Chapter 11

Alan tore out the door after her. Antonia heard him shout behind her, but she was already off the porch in a single leap and headed toward the car when Alan came tearing out the front door, shouting at her to come back.

Thankful that she had given up locking her car in this small town, she ran around the front of the car and hopped in, slamming the lock down just as Alan reached her car. He grabbed at the door handle on the passenger side, and when he found it locked, he slapped the window hard. Antonia was fumbling to put her key in the ignition, her breath coming in sobs in her throat. Tears of fear and anger were running down her face, and her hands shook.

"Damn you!" Alan raged, crashing his fist into the window. He did it again, and the window cracked.

Antonia got the key into the ignition and turned it,

jerking the SUV into gear and gunning it backward. Alan jumped back, cursing, then turned and ran toward his own car. Antonia whipped into the street, slammed on her brakes, then zoomed forward.

She streaked down the empty residential street, glancing up into her rearview mirror to see what Alan was doing. She saw his headlights come on as she zipped around a corner, the bulky vehicle wobbling a little. Keeping a watch on the rearview mirror, she turned right again at the next block and pushed the accelerator down. In her mirror, she saw Alan's car go tearing past the intersection. She made an immediate right and headed north, streaking through the quiet streets of town toward the highway.

She still had not seen any headlights in her rearview mirror by the time she reached the highway and turned left. Her SUV might not corner well, but it had plenty of power, and she took full advantage of it, jamming down on the accelerator. She blasted out of town, not caring if a policeman stopped her. Frankly, she wished one of Quinn's men would appear out of nowhere and pull her over.

None did, however, and neither did any other car come onto the road behind her. She raced along the straight, flat highway, the speedometer zooming up toward ninety. She was sure she had lost Alan, and he would have no idea where she was going. But she could not bring herself to slow down. Without any conscious thought, she was fleeing to Daniel.

By the time she reached the turn-off to his farm, she was shaking so hard from an overflow of adrenaline that she had to try twice to punch the numbers in at the gate. The whole time she kept glancing over her shoulder, as if Alan might magically appear behind her. When the gate opened, she shot through, kicking up dust and bouncing over the ruts in bone-jarring fashion.

She pulled to a stop in front of the house and jumped out, not even bothering to turn off her headlights. She ran to the porch and up the steps. Just as she reached the door, the porch light came on and the door opened. Daniel stood there, looking surprised and worried, shoes off and shirt unbuttoned, obviously already headed for bed.

"Antonia?" He opened the screen door for her, and Antonia threw herself into his arms. "Sweetheart? What's the matter? Are you crying? You're shaking like a leaf. What happened?"

"Alan! Oh, God, Daniel! It was Alan." His arms were blessedly warm and safe around her, and Antonia clung to him as if she could absorb his strength and calm.

"Alan? You mean, you ex?" His arms tightened around her. "You saw him? He's here?"

Antonia nodded. "Yes. He came to the house after you left. I thought it was you coming back and I opened the door without looking. It was stupid, but it's been so long.... I'm sorry. I'm a mess. I can't seem to stop shaking."

"Don't worry about that. You're okay now. You're safe." He leaned his head against hers, his arms encircling her securely. "Did he hurt you? I'll kill the son of a bitch."

"He didn't hurt me," Antonia said quickly. "Well,

I mean, he grabbed my arm, but he didn't hit me or anything. I ran away. I was so scared! I threw a cup of coffee in his face and ran."

Daniel smiled. "That's my girl."

"Dad? What's the matter? What's going on?" James appeared in the doorway, clad only in boxers and rubbing his head sleepily. "Oh! Dr. Campbell!" He stepped back, looking embarrassed.

"It's okay, son. Go on back to bed."

"But what—"

Daniel jerked his head expressively toward the rest of the house, and James grimaced, but turned and left. Daniel curled his arm around Antonia and walked her into the family room. He sat down in his large, comfortable chair and pulled her into his lap, cradling her against him. Antonia snuggled up, the side of her face against his chest, listening to the steady, reassuring thump of his heart, letting his warmth wrap around her and soothe her.

They sat like that for a long time, until finally Antonia's trembling stopped and she no longer felt chilled to the bone. Finally, Daniel spoke, "Okay. You feeling better?"

Antonia nodded.

"Can you tell me exactly what happened?"

"Right after you left, the doorbell rang, and I thought it was you, coming back for some reason. So I went to the door and didn't even look out the peephole, just opened the door. It was Alan. I froze for a moment, and then I slammed the door, but he was already halfway in, and I couldn't close it. He came in. He said he wanted to talk. He said—" She stopped.

She could feel the shaking coming back just at the memory. She clenched her teeth together for a second and went on. ''He said he wanted to try again. He wanted me to come back to Virginia with him. Apparently he was close by somewhere tonight. He saw you bring me home and leave, because he asked if I was dating you. I don't know how long he's been here, spying on me....''

She could not suppress a shiver at the thought of Alan having been there, hanging around the edges of her life, watching her, without her knowing it. That was even worse than the phone calls, which could have been made from anywhere.

''It's okay,'' Daniel told her, smoothing his hand over her back in a slow, soothing circle. ''He's not going to do anything else to you.''

''It's so awful—to think of him watching me without my knowing. You know?''

''Yeah. I know. Did he threaten you?''

''No. He acted reasonable until the very end. That's always the way he is. He told me he was sorry and all that sort of thing, and told me how he wanted another chance. That's typical of him. But I was scared to be there with him, so I managed to get my keys so I could get away from him if I needed to. Thank God I did, because when I told him that I wasn't going back to him, ever, that I didn't love him, he began to get angry.''

''What did he do?'' Daniel asked, his voice low and tight.

''Nothing, really. He grabbed my arm, and he kind of shook me. But the way he looked—the way he sounded—I knew it was going to get worse. He wouldn't let go of my arm. So I hit him with my coffee cup and ran for the car."

"Good for you. Grabbing your arm and shaking you is plenty. He won't do it again. I promise you."

Antonia sighed and leaned her head against Daniel's chest again. Her eyelids were heavy, and her brain felt foggy and numb. She had often felt that way before after a stressful situation, as though her whole system were shutting down. "I'm sorry. I'm so tired all of a sudden."

"Of course you are." Daniel kissed the top of her head. "Just go to sleep."

"I'll have to get an injunction against him here."

"Sure. And you'll stay here till he's taken care of."

Antonia thought foggily that she probably should not stay. But she didn't have the strength to protest. Besides, she knew there was no way she could go back to her home tonight. *Being strong and independent would have to wait.* Her eyelids drifted closed, and, lulled by the warmth and safety of Daniel's arms, she fell asleep.

Daniel sat holding her for a long time until he was sure she was deeply asleep. Then he rose and carried her up the stairs to his room. Gently he laid her down on his bed. Antonia stirred a little, but her eyes did not open, and she sank back into a deep sleep. He took off her shoes and pulled the comforter over her. For a long moment he stood looking down at her, before he turned and walked softly from the room, closing the door after him.

He went down the hall to James's room. He found

his son sitting on his bed, dressed now, and restlessly cracking his knuckles. James jumped up anxiously. "What's going on? What's the matter with Antonia?"

"Her ex-husband came to visit her tonight. It scared her, so she came out here."

"It scared her? Why? Is he—I mean, did he used to—"

"Yeah. He used to knock her around. That's why she came to Texas in the first place. He wasn't supposed to know where she was, but somehow he found out."

James frowned. "He didn't hurt her, did he?"

"No thanks to him. She got away before he could. I'm going to take care of it."

"I'll go with you."

"No. You have to stay here. Somebody's got to be here in case Antonia wakes up. I don't want her to be alone."

"All right," James agreed reluctantly.

"Thanks."

He left the room, with James on his heels, and went downstairs to the kitchen. There he dialed Quinn's number. When Quinn didn't answer, he dialed his father's house, where Quinn was still hanging out with Cater and Cory, enjoying the remnants of the Fourth of July party.

"Hey, Quinn, I need a favor," Daniel began without preamble.

"Shoot." Quinn sounded faintly surprised.

"I need to find out if someone is staying at the motel."

"Here in Angel Eye? Why? Who are you talking about?"

"Antonia's ex." He gave him a short synopsis of what had happened.

"This guy used to rough her up?" Quinn asked. "Maybe I ought to pay him a visit."

"No. I want to handle it myself. I just want to find out if he's staying at the motel. He's been following Antonia, apparently, spying on her, so I'm thinking he's probably staying here, didn't just drive in today. Anyway, I don't figure the Lodge would give out that kind of information to me. But they would to you. His name is Alan Brent, and he's from Virginia, so my guess is he's here in a rental car, or maybe one with Virginia plates."

"He could be staying in Hammond," Quinn pointed out. "I'll check there, too. Call you back as soon as I find anything out."

Daniel sat down to wait, and James took a seat across the table from him. Daniel's face was cold and set, and neither of them spoke. Time passed with excruciating slowness.

Finally the telephone shrilled, cutting through the silence, and Daniel grabbed it. "Yeah?"

"Got it. He's registered at the Angel Eye Lodge, room 14. Checked in yesterday. Horace says he's in his room now."

"Thanks."

"Listen, Daniel..." Quinn said, a cautionary note in his voice. "You aren't going to do anything I'm going to have to arrest you for, are you?"

"I don't plan to kill him, if that's what you mean."

"Good. You want me to come with you? Cater and Cory are here, too."

A faint smile tugged at the corner of Daniel's mouth. "Thanks. But I can handle it. Bye."

Daniel hung up the phone and turned to his son. "I'm leaving now. If Antonia wakes up, tell her I'll be right back."

"Okay." James looked longingly toward the door. "Are you sure—"

"I need you here," Daniel replied firmly.

James sighed. "All right. Be careful."

Daniel smiled in a chilling way that his son had never seen. "Oh, you don't need to worry about me. It's that son-of-a-bitch Brent who needs to worry."

Daniel turned and walked out the door.

Daniel knocked on the motel door and waited, schooling his face into an expressionless mask. After a moment, the door opened to reveal an innocuous-looking man a few inches shorter than Daniel.

"Yes?"

"Alan Brent?"

"Yes." The man frowned. "Who—" Even as he spoke, recognition lit his features, and he stepped back quickly, shutting the door.

Daniel threw his full weight against the door before it latched and shoved it open, throwing Alan backward. He stumbled and fell to the floor. Daniel strode forward and grabbed him by the front of his shirt, jerking him to his feet.

"Looks like you recognized me," Daniel said, bar-ing his teeth in a travesty of a smile. "Been sneaking around following Antonia on her dates, huh?"

"I don't know what you're talking about," the other man replied. "Let go of me, or I'll have the police on you."

"Oh, I doubt that," Daniel said genially. "Seeing as how my brother is the sheriff, I don't think you'd get real far with that one. I suggest you sit down now, and let's have us a little talk."

He shoved Alan backward so that he sat down hard on the bed. Alan immediately bounced back up, his face reddening with anger. "See here, you oaf, I—"

Daniel swung his fist, connecting with Alan's solar plexus, and the air went out of him in a great rush. He fell back on the bed, doubled up and gasping for air.

"Talky bastard, aren't you? You just shut up for a minute, and let me tell you what I came to say. I drove over here thinking about how I was going to beat the hell out of you...give you a little taste of what it feels like to be on the receiving end instead of dishing it out. Not too good, huh? But then I figured, why put the doctors and nurses to the trouble and all? I mean, I realized, a guy like you, who beats up women, is pretty much a coward and a blowhard, you know? I mean, if you were really a tough guy, you would get into fights where the odds were more even. That's what I'm thinking. So I figured that a warning would probably do it for you."

Daniel leaned closer, asking conversationally, "What do you think? You going to go quietly? Or are you going to give me the opportunity to beat you like a drum?"

"That bitch!" Alan shoved himself off the bed, his face contorted with fury.

Daniel sidestepped the other man's charge, sending a short, powerful jab into Alan's ribs as the man went past. Alan reeled, and Daniel went after him, sending an uppercut into his chin, followed by another short blow to the stomach. Alan collapsed onto the floor. Daniel reached down, grabbed him by the collar and hauled him to his feet.

"Damn it!" he snapped, his face only inches from Alan's, his black eyes glittering coldly. "I hear one more thing like that from you and it'll be the last time anyone hears your voice for weeks. Do I make myself clear?"

Alan nodded, gasping and gagging, tears of pain in his eyes.

"Doesn't feel so good, does it?" Daniel asked coldly. "When you're the one being the punching bag? Well, let me tell you something. You could feel a lot worse—and you will, if you don't do what I tell you to right now. When I leave here, you are going to pack your bags and get in that car and drive like hell out of this town. And you are never coming back here. You are also never calling Antonia on the phone again. Or writing her or anything else. 'Cause if you do—if you come here, if you try to contact her in any way—then I'm coming after you. And next time I won't stop until you've learned your lesson."

He paused, then added, "You know, I've been castrating calves since I was twelve years old, and I'm real good at it. You might want to think about that."

Daniel relaxed his grip on Alan's shirt and let him

fall onto the bed. "Have we reached an agreement here?"

"Yes!" Alan hissed. "Now get out."

"I will. But in one hour I'm phoning Horace. He's the one running the front desk here, and I'm going to ask him if you've checked out and left. And if you haven't, I'm coming back down here."

"All right! All right! Just leave."

At that moment the door to the room swung back, and Quinn stepped into the room. "You left the door open," he said pleasantly. "That's real careless. A person could get himself hurt that way."

Alan looked up from his position on the bed, his face going white with sheer terror as four more men filed into the room after Quinn, each one seemingly taller than the one before him, and each wearing a similarly grim expression.

Daniel turned to his brother. "Hey, Quinn." He glanced at the others and shook his head. "You guys just couldn't resist, could you? James, what the hell are you doing here? What if Antonia wakes up?"

"Beth's with her. She came with Quinn and them."

"We thought you could use a little help," Cory offered, then glanced at the man on the bed. "I can see that wasn't necessary."

Daniel rolled his eyes.

"Actually, Cater and Cory were just wanting to get in on the fun," Quinn explained. He, too, looked at Alan disparagingly. "Doesn't look like it lasted long."

"No, not really. Mr. Brent's just about to pack up and leave Angel Eye."

"That's too bad," Quinn said with regret. "I was

planning to talk to Antonia tomorrow about pressing charges. I figure assault—''

''I didn't touch her!'' Alan protested, sitting up gingerly.

Quinn shrugged. ''Not what I heard. Assault. Stalking. That'll be enough to arrest you, I think. I could use some company down at the jail.'' He grinned at Alan in a way that was enough to chill one's blood. ''Oddest things happen in jails sometimes. Prisoners hurting themselves...having accidents...getting into fights...''

Alan stared at him speechlessly.

''Oh well,'' Quinn continued conversationally. ''Probably better all around if you left Angel Eye, though. Antonia might not want folks knowing what a sleaze her ex is. Provided you don't come back, of course. 'Cause if you do, your ass'll be in jail the first day. That's a promise.''

Alan nodded. Quinn glanced around the room. ''Guess we might as well leave. Daniel? You coming?''

Daniel turned. He quirked an eyebrow at his brother. ''Worried? If I was going to do anything worse to him, I would have already.''

''Is that it?'' Cory asked, sounding aggrieved.

Cater snorted. ''What do you want to do?''

''I don't know.'' Cory sighed. ''I just thought there would be more of a fight.''

''Well, there might have been if I had been a woman,'' Daniel replied sarcastically. He turned and started for the door. ''Come on, guys. I think I'm done here.''

* * *

Antonia awakened groggily. Her head ached, and her eyes were swollen from crying. She blinked, looking around her, disoriented. It took a moment to realize where she was and another moment to remember why. Then she groaned, her stomach clenching, as she recalled the scene with Alan and her flight to Daniel's house. *She had run to Daniel like a frightened child, looking for protection!* Shame and self-anger swept her at the memory. She had worked so hard for so many years to become a strong, independent person, and she'd thought she had succeeded. *Then, as soon as Alan reappeared in her life, she had returned to that silly, frightened person she had once been, running to Daniel.*

She sat up, burying her face in her hands. Alan had managed to humiliate her again by exposing her weakness, and she hated him for it. Finally, she sighed, running her fingers back through her hair, and got out of her bed. She made the bed. She couldn't tell if Daniel had slept there last night or not. The last thing she remembered was falling asleep in Daniel's arms downstairs. *Like a baby.*

She shook her head, pushing away the thought, and went to the mirror to assess the damage. The mirror confirmed that her eyes were puffy and red-rimmed from crying, and her hair was a mess. A folded pair of jeans and a T-shirt had been laid on the dresser, and she smiled a little at Daniel's thoughtfulness, her eyes filling up with tears. She wiped the tears away irritatedly, thinking she was a real mess, and took the clothes into the adjoining bathroom. She took a long, hot shower, and by the time she got out, she felt somewhat revived.

It was not the end of the world, she reminded herself. She could take control of her life again. She would return home, for one thing, despite the fear that shot through her at the thought. She would have an extra bolt put on both the front and back doors, and make sure that her windows were as secure as they possibly could be. And she would go to a lawyer, no matter how embarrassing it would be to tell some stranger the sordid details of her first marriage, and get him to file for an injunction against Alan, forbidding him to contact her. She would protect herself, but she would not give in to the fear that gnawed at her. Alan might be lurking around her house; he might call her or harass her. She knew she would be looking around for him every time she left the house. But the important thing was that she would show him she was not afraid of him. She would go on with her life as normal.

Thus resolved, she felt somewhat better. She combed out her hair and dressed in the jeans and T-shirt Daniel had left. The jeans must have belonged to James, from the narrowness of their hips, so they didn't fit her too badly, except that they were several inches too long. She rolled up the cuffs to her ankles and thought she looked at least passable.

She went down the stairs. She could hear noises from the direction of the kitchen, so she went toward it. Daniel was at the stove, pancakes on a griddle before him. He turned at the sound of her approach and smiled.

“Hey, there. How you feeling? Pancakes sound good?”

“They sound great.” Antonia hesitated at the doorway, feeling a little awkward.

“I called the clinic this morning and told them you wouldn’t be in today. I said you were feeling sick.”

“What? The clinic? Oh.” She had forgotten that today was a work day, since the Fourth had fallen in the middle of the week. “I see. I—uh, thanks.” She wondered what Lilian would think about Daniel calling in for her so early in the morning. She would probably be shocked to her toes. Antonia wished that Daniel had not done that; she would have preferred to call in herself. But she could hardly gripe when he had been trying to help her out.

“I—I’m sorry,” she said, going back to what she had intended to say when she came into the kitchen.

“For what?”

“For crashing in on you like that last night.”

“That’s okay.” Daniel looked puzzled. “Where else would you go?”

“I should have handled it myself. I could have gone to the police or driven into Hammond to stay.” Her keys were on the table, and she picked them up and stuck them in her pocket, remembering a little shamefacedly the way she had tumbled out of the truck and run in here. She had left the lights on; it was a wonder she had even remembered to take the keys out of the ignition.

Daniel lifted the pancakes and plopped them down on a plate, turned off the stove, and carried the plate of pancakes to the table. “We can still go to the cops if you want. Quinn would be happy to put out a warrant for that guy. But I don't think you have to worry about your ex anymore. He won't be coming back." He set the plate down and came around the table to pull her into his arms. He kissed the top of her head.

Antonia pulled back and looked up at him. "What do you mean, he won't be coming back? How do you know? Daniel...what happened?"

"Nothing much." He shrugged and walked over to one of the cabinets, taking out plates and cups. "I went to see him and told him to stop bothering you. And he left town."

"Wait. Hold on." Antonia stared at him, stunned. She felt as if someone had just knocked the air out of her, "Are you telling me you confronted Alan? About his coming over to my house last night?"

"Sure. What else would I do?"

"What happened? What did you do?"

"I hit him."

"You hit him? Are you saying you beat him up?"

"Well, yeah, a little, I guess."

"You beat him up a *little? You guess?*"

"Yeah. I hit him a few times. What's the matter?" He looked at her oddly. "Why are you looking at me like that? You think I was going to let him terrorize you and do nothing?"

"I certainly didn't think you were going to resort to the same kind of brutal behavior he engages in!" Antonia retorted hotly. "How could you?"

"You're comparing me to him?" Daniel's voice rose in astonishment and the beginnings of anger. "Are you serious?"

"Of course I'm serious. He hurts me, so you hurt him. He threatens me, so you threaten him. How does that make you different?"

Daniel's face went blank, and he stepped back. "You can't see the difference between what I did and what he did? I have never hurt a woman in my life."

"But you have no compunction about reverting to brute force to get your way, do you?"

"I wasn't just getting my way!" Daniel retorted. "Good God, Antonia! I was protecting you. I went over there to make sure he didn't hurt you again—ever. It's not like I'm in the habit of beating people up just because they do something I don't like. But no way *am* I going to stand around and let him hurt you."

Anger shot through Antonia like a wildfire. "Oh, so you have to go out and protect the poor little female who's incapable of protecting herself. Is that it? Pack me off to bed, where I'll be out of your way, then go off like a caveman to protect your territory!"

"Damn it, Antonia, you're twisting this all around."

"I don't have to twist it. It seems pretty clear to me that you took it upon yourself to clear up my problems for me. I can handle them myself, thank you very much. I don't need you or any other man going out and 'taking care of me.' I am a grown woman and quite capable of standing on my own two feet."

"I never said—"

"You didn't have to say anything. Your actions speak for you. It's obvious that you didn't think I could handle it. That you thought you had to do it for me."

"That's not true."

"Oh, please..." Antonia turned away, crossing her arms over her chest and hugging them to her. She was churning with emotions, faintly sick with them.

"This is crazy," Daniel said, his voice vibrating with frustration.

"How did you find him?" Antonia asked. "How did you even know where to go?"

"Quinn helped me there. He called the Lodge and asked if he was staying there."

"Quinn? You told your brother about it?"

"Well, yeah. I needed his help. I had to find out where Alan was, and quick. I might could have gotten the folks at the Lodge to tell me if he was there, but not any of the motels in Hammond, and he could have been staying there. But Quinn could find out."

"So you revealed my innermost secrets, the things I told you in confidence, to your brother? The one who you say talks so much? The one with the dispatcher who's Gossip Central? Everyone in town will know all about it tomorrow! Oh, God, I'll be embarrassed to see any of my patients!"

"He won't spread it around," Daniel protested. "I mean, yeah, Quinn can talk, but he wouldn't reveal an important secret. He's the sheriff, for heaven's sake. Not to mention the fact that he's family."

"He's not *my* family!"

"You were just talking about going to the cops. Who do you think you would be talking to? Quinn, that's who. What's the difference?"

"That's precisely why I was reluctant to go to him."

"Why? Why do you feel the need to protect that little twirp?"

"What? Protect Alan? I'm not protecting Alan."

"You could have fooled me," Daniel told her, cold anger lacing his voice. "You don't want me making him leave town and stop harassing you. You don't want to go to the sheriff because he's my brother. I don't see how that benefits anyone except Alan Brent."

"It's not like that at all. I am not trying to protect Alan! I'm just trying to maintain a little privacy. I don't care to have my whole sordid past laid out before everyone."

"My brothers aren't 'everyone.'"

"Brothers?" Antonia asked sharply, one eyebrow lifting. "Plural?"

"Yeah."

"You told *all* your brothers?"

Daniel looked uncomfortable. "No. They were over at Dad's house with Quinn when I called. So when Quinn came after me to make sure I didn't kill the guy or something, Cater and Cory insisted on coming with him. Alan had already said he would leave and never bother you again. But Quinn came in at the end and added a little weight to it, being the sheriff and all."

"So all your brothers added their bit of intimidation to yours."

Daniel shrugged. "I guess you could say that."

"I can't believe this." Antonia threw up her hands.

"I don't understand why you're so upset."

"You don't understand why I'm upset? You took over my life. You sent me to bed, then went out and fixed everything up without even telling me one thing about what you were going to do. You didn't ask me. You didn't tell me. You just took control. Not only that, your idea of fixing things is to force someone else to do what you want by intimidation and violence!''

''I just did what I had to do,'' Daniel said, setting his jaw stubbornly. ''What any man in my position would.''

''No, not any man,'' Antonia retorted heatedly. ''Not any man who respected me and my thoughts and feelings. You didn't ask me what I wanted. What I needed. You did what *you* figured was best for me. The same way you decided to call the clinic this morning and tell them I wasn't coming in because I was sick. You didn't ask me. You just did it. You assumed that *you* were best suited to make those decisions about my life, not me.''

''It wasn't like that!''

''No? I'm afraid I have a little trouble seeing the difference.'' Antonia turned and strode away. She could feel the tears beating at the backs of her eyes, but she refused to break down and cry in front of him. She was furious. Disappointed.

''Antonia!'' Daniel started after her.

She whirled to face him. ''No! I don't want to talk to you right now. I'm not sure I want to talk to you ever again!''

''Antonia! You don't mean that!''

''Don't tell me what I mean! I meant exactly what I said.'' Her eyes filled with tears, and she blinked them away. ''How could I possibly marry a man who tried to run my life for me? I swore that I'd never let myself get into that kind of situation again."

Daniel stiffened and went white. "That is the second time you've compared me to that animal you married. Is that what you think of me?"

"I think that I made a terrible mistake by letting things go this far. I can't marry you. I can't marry anyone. I knew I couldn't, and I was stupid to—" Antonia clamped her lips together, fighting to hold back her tears. She swallowed hard. "Goodbye, Daniel. I'm sorry."

"Antonia!" He started after her, reaching out for her, then stopped and shoved his hands into his pockets. He stood, watching her leave, despair and confusion mingling on his face.

Antonia made it to the SUV before the tears began to fall. She turned the ignition, threw the vehicle into gear and rattled off down the dirt driveway, crying as if her heart would break.

Chapter 12

Antonia drove home and rushed into her house. Slamming the front door and locking it, she ran into her bedroom and threw herself on the bed in a fit of tears. Mitzi, lying in her usual spot in the chair, jumped off and leapt up onto the bed. She padded up to Antonia and looked at her for a moment, then curled up close beside her.

Antonia lay on her bed crying for a long time, and after that she lay there in a numbed state for even longer. The telephone rang, but she ignored it. It was afternoon before she finally sat up and looked around her. It occurred to her that she had not even checked out the rest of the house for signs that Alan had returned—even though the front door had been unlocked and open a few inches, left that way by their headlong rush from the house yesterday. Anyone could have come in, including her ex-husband or someone else or any number of four-legged animals. It was amazing, she thought, how misery disposed of fear.

She got up and walked through the house now, the cat padding along behind her, halfheartedly checking all around to make sure that all the windows and doors were locked and that no animals had gotten in. She wandered back into the living room and plopped down on the couch. Her head was throbbing, and her eyes felt the size of baseballs. She thought about getting a cold wet rag to cover her eyes, but it seemed appropriate that she should feel this awful when her life was in ruins around her.

It was her own fault, of course. She had let herself fall in love, despite all her intentions to the contrary. And look what had happened.

For a brief while she had been happy—happier than she could remember ever being. But because she had been so happy, she had not been careful. She hadn't been watchful. She had slipped and fallen in love with him. *Why, she had thought yesterday that she would say yes to Daniel's marriage proposal.* She knew better. Daniel had become too important to her, too integral a part of her life. The longer she was around him, the more important he would become, until she was lost in him, unable to live without him.

Antonia could not allow herself to become that weak, dependent person again.

Daniel had already proved that he would do as he pleased without even consulting her. He was quite ready to make decisions for her, to take over her life. He was different from Alan in that he wanted to wrap her up in protective swaddling rather than use her as a whipping boy for all his problems. But the result would be the same; he would control her life.

Right now she still had the strength to resist him, to argue with him and prevent him from taking over. She was an individual, a person, and she would stand up for herself with him. But if she married him, she was afraid that she would sink into a swamp of dependency—her identity, her self, even her will, given up to him. The prospect filled her with terror.

No, she assured herself, she had done the right thing. She could not marry Daniel. This way, she might be miserable, but at least she would be her own person.

Antonia went to bed early. It seemed as though it would be heaven to fall asleep and let go of all her thoughts and emotions. However, when she lay down, she found that she was unable to go to sleep. She kept thinking of Daniel, recalling their conversation, going over her decision, and every time she did, she wound up wiping tears away. She would have said she had no tears left after her crying bout this morning, but obviously she would have been wrong.

It seemed as if she had hardly closed her eyes before her alarm went off the next morning. Reluctantly, she pulled herself out of bed and stumbled through her morning shower and a cup of coffee. She dressed as she always did, in slacks and a plain, serviceable shirt, both beige, and tied her hair back in a low knot on the nape of her neck. She looked at herself in the mirror and noted that she looked all one color—clothes, hair, skin—except for the prominent dark circles beneath her eyes. However, she did not have the energy to change clothes or put on makeup. Anyway, she reasoned, the animals wouldn't care.

Rita Delgado was sitting at the technicians' station, writing on a chart, when Antonia came in the side door. She looked up at Antonia, and her eyes widened.

"Antonia! Are you all right?" Rita stood up and came toward her. "Maybe you should have stayed at home today. You look like you still don't feel well."

"Oh." Antonia remembered that Daniel had said he used illness as an excuse when he'd called the clinic yesterday to say that she would not be coming in. "No. I'm all right. Really."

Rita frowned. "If you say so. But I'm thinking maybe you ought to turn around and go back home."

"No." The thought of spending another day moping around her house, unable to sleep and unable to do anything but think about Daniel, gave her the shivers. "I need to work. I mean, I want to. Just let me get a cup of coffee and I'll be fine."

She went to the break room. Lilian was just leaving with a mug of coffee as Antonia went in, and she looked at Antonia curiously. Antonia wasn't sure if it was because she looked so haggard or because she was scandalized that Daniel had called in sick for Antonia yesterday morning. She shrugged, not feeling up to worrying about something as small as her reputation right now, and poured herself a cup of coffee. She returned to her office to catch up on a bit of paperwork before her first appointment, but she found it difficult to concentrate. Stubbornly, she plowed ahead, making little progress.

The phone rang, and when she answered it, Lilian, the receptionist, said, "You have a call, line one. He says it's an emergency, but he won't say who it is."

Antonia sighed. "Is it Daniel?"

"Oh, no, I'd recognize his voice. It's someone else."

"Okay. Put him through."

A moment later, a furious male voice shrieked through the earpiece at her, "You bitch! You sneaky, deceitful, slutty little bitch!"

"Alan?" Antonia asked wearily. She felt too depressed and tired to summon up even a quiver of fear at the sound of him. "I'm surprised you're calling me here. Couldn't you get the new home number?"

"You think you're so clever, you and that Neanderthal cowboy of yours. Well, I have news for him. I'm going to sue the hell out of him. He'll regret the day he ever decided to lock horns with me."

"Oh, grow up, Alan," Antonia snapped, a little amazed to find that the primary emotion she was experiencing was irritation. "I can file charges against you for breaking into my house and assaulting me."

"I barely touched you."

"Touch is enough, Alan. You're a lawyer. You know that. Grabbing my arm and shaking me certainly qualifies. I can get an injunction forbidding you to come near me. That will really impress a jury when you sue Daniel. This is a little town in Texas, Alan. The jury won't be impressed by your bruises. They'll just think you're a wimp. They do, however, know Daniel and his family. They're one of the founding families of the county. And given the testimony of his brother, the *sheriff,* you'll be lucky if they don't decide to make *you* pay *him.*"

"They're a bunch of hicks."

"Do you really want to hire an attorney in Texas and come all this way just to look like a fool in front of a bunch of hicks?"

Antonia could almost hear Alan's teeth grinding, and she felt a perverse spurt of good cheer.

"That's it. You've had your last chance," Alan went on, his voice on the verge of a whine. "You'll never see me again."

"Good."

"You could have had a good life. I was willing to take you back. But it's too late now. I'm through with you. There are plenty of women here who would be happy to marry me."

"I feel sorry for them."

"Enjoy your life among the cow pies," Alan said acidly before he broke the connection.

Antonia replaced the receiver on its hook and sat back. Alan had been full of bluff and bluster; she could hear it in his voice. She knew that he would not come after her again. Daniel had humiliated him. If he could have, he would have made her pay for it physically, but she could also hear the undercurrent of fear and shame in his voice, and she knew that he didn't have the nerve to return. Nor, she thought, would he even want to see her again, not with her knowing about his humiliation. The knowledge was wonderfully freeing.

Her first thought was to pick up the phone again and call Daniel, but she froze as she reached for the receiver, then let her hand fall back to the desk. Calling Daniel was not something she could do anymore.

The next few days crept by, sweltering and slow. Daniel called Antonia again and again, both at home and at her office, but she avoided the calls. She knew she should talk to him, should explain better why she had had to end their relationship, but she was afraid she would not be able to get through the conversation without bursting into tears. She also knew, uneasily, that Daniel was all too likely to present his argument in such a way that she would not be able to resist. *And that was precisely why she had had to stop seeing him!* He was able to sway her far too easily.

She was finding it terribly difficult not to see him, though. She had known it would hurt, but she had not realized just how much. It seemed as if a multitude of things happened every day that she wanted to tell Daniel about. She was lonely, lonelier than she could ever remember being. She wanted to kiss him, to feel his arms around her, to hear the reassuring rumble of his voice. At all hours of the day, thoughts of him would come to her—the lazy warmth of his smile, the way his eyes crinkled at the corners, the hair that would flop down onto his forehead as he worked, the strength of his hands, the sexy line of his legs in blue jeans and boots.

Everything seemed to conspire to remind her of him. She couldn't go into the Moonstone Café without thinking of the first time they'd eaten there together. She couldn't even walk the aisles of the grocery store without remembering the times they had gone in together to pick up something for supper. She saw James crossing the street in front of the post office one day, and she was pierced by a pain so harsh that she thought she would die from it. One day Quinn came to the clinic to see her, and just the sight of him made her want to cry. He was quiet and polite, without his usual laughing demeanor, and she was sure that he hated her. His whole family must hate her. For the first time in fifteen years, Daniel had fallen in love again, and she had rejected him. They would not understand her reasons, she knew; neither would she, in their place.

"Hello, Quinn." She rose a little shakily.

"Ma'am." He took off his hat. "I thought I would let you know what I've found out. I know you didn't file charges, but Daniel asked me to look into it, so I did. We think we know how Alan Brent tracked you down."

"Oh?" Antonia no longer really cared. Her mother had sworn that she had not told him where Antonia lived, and Antonia had believed her.

"The vet where you used to work in Katy. When we talked to them, the receptionist finally remembered that A&M had called, wanting to know your new address. But when I contacted the university, their records department denied ever calling. I suspect it was Brent or some detective he hired."

Antonia nodded. "All right. Well, I...thank you."

"I know it doesn't make much difference now. I don't think that office will be giving out any more information about you without checking first, though."

"I don't think he will try again." Antonia's fingers curled up into fists. She wished he would leave. It was too painful to look at him, to see the similarity in his mouth and nose and the shape of his face.

Quinn nodded and turned to go. He stopped, then swung back. "Antonia..."

"Yes?"

"He never meant any harm, you know. Daniel's a good man. He—maybe he made a mistake. We always tell people it's a mistake to take the law into their own hands. But he was sick with worry about you. He wanted to protect you."

Antonia nodded, blinking back the tears that sprang into her eyes. "I know."

"He's miserable without you."

Antonia clenched her fists, digging her nails into her palms, to keep from crying. She swallowed hard. "Thank you."

He sighed, nodded and left the room. Antonia sat back down at her desk, covering her face with her hands, and once again the tears came.

She hated thinking that she had hurt Daniel. She knew that he had done what he thought was right. She hated the way she hurt, too. Her whole life seemed in shambles. In less than three months Daniel had become such a huge part of her life, so important, that his absence left a gaping hole in it.

Every night she cried herself to sleep in her empty bed, often after having listened to the hang-up after hang-up on her answering machine that she knew were calls from Daniel. It was hard to work up any interest in eating. She had difficulty sleeping, and the dark circles under her eyes seemed in danger of becoming permanent.

She could see the people with whom she worked looking at her in concern. One afternoon, as she left an examining room, Rita Delgado pounced on her and whisked her off into the employee lounge, where she closed and locked the door behind them. She turned to face Antonia, crossing her arms across her chest.

“Okay,” she said firmly. “Tell me what's going on.”

“Rita…”

“I'm not telling anyone else, I promise you. I don't have any interest in gossiping about this. But I know that everybody is saying that you and Daniel Sutton aren't seeing each other anymore, and I know that he's called up here at least ten times this week and you won't talk to him. And I know that you look like hell.”

“Thank you very much.”

“Come on, Antonia, I'm serious. What happened? My nephew told me you dumped Daniel.”

“I didn't dump him!” Antonia protested. “I—I just decided not to see him anymore.”

“I think I'm missing the distinction.”

“Well, there is one,” Antonia said a trifle sullenly.

“Look,” Rita said, in as serious a tone as Antonia had ever heard her use. “I don't know what happened, and obviously you don't plan to talk about it. But whatever your reasons are for not seeing Daniel again, I think you better ask yourself—are they worth all this pain?”

Rita gave her a tap on the arm for emphasis, then

walked out. Antonia leaned back against the wall, suddenly swamped with the misery that never seemed to be very far away from her these days. It was some time before she was able to straighten and leave to go to the next examining room.

The chart that was sitting in the holder on the door did not lift her spirits any. The patient was an eight-year-old Lhasa apso named Buster, a corker of a dog whom Antonia had already decided was personally out to get her. He was the beloved pet of Mrs. Kritzer, seventy-five years old and plenty feisty herself, and though Buster was one of the healthiest animals Antonia had ever treated, his owner was convinced that he suffered from a series of maladies and brought him in frequently.

Antonia pasted a smile on her face and went inside. "Hello, Mrs. Kritzer. How are you today?"

"I'm fine, Dr. Campbell," the old lady responded. "But it's time for Buster's shots, I'm afraid." She sighed and looked down at Buster, who was sitting on the examining table with Rita on one side of him and Mrs. Kritzer on the other. "Poor thing."

Buster regarded Antonia with bright black button eyes, and Antonia was sure that he was preparing himself for a series of twists and curls worthy of a rodeo bronc when she tried to give him his shots.

Antonia moved toward the examining table, saying, "You need to sit down, Mrs. Kritzer. It's better if Mrs. Delgado and I hold Buster on the examining table."

"But Buster is so scared when I'm not there," the older woman said plaintively.

Antonia determinedly did not look toward her assistant, for fear that she would not be able to keep a straight face as she said, "Mrs. Kritzer, Buster knows that you're here with him even if you aren't holding him, and that will make him feel safe."

In Antonia's opinion, Buster would not be afraid of the Devil himself. In fact, most people who knew Buster believed that the dog was actually a close relation to Beelzebub. But she said only, "He'll be fine, Mrs. Kritzer, I promise you."

"If you're sure..."

"I am."

Antonia examined the dog quickly and competently, then took the syringe that Rita handed her. Rita took a firm grip of the dog's head and shoulders. Antonia clamped down on his backside with equal determination and quickly administered the shot.

It was over before Buster, braced to squirm and wriggle, got a chance to begin. Antonia let go, and Rita relaxed her grip, and Buster cast Antonia an irritated look for ruining his act.

"There you go. Not even a yelp. Good dog, Buster." Antonia rubbed him behind his ears. Buster regarded her balefully.

Mrs. Kritzer rose from her chair and came to Buster's head, petting him, and clucking and cooing over him. Buster leaned his head against her pitifully, wriggling his back end. "There, there, sweetums," Mrs. Kritzer assured him. "It's all over now."

"Buster's left ear looked a little red today, Mrs. Kritzer," Antonia went on as she went to the sink to wash her hands. "So I am going to give you some drops to put in—"

She stopped short, toweling her hands dry, as the door to the examining room opened suddenly. Daniel stood in the doorway. Behind him, she could hear footsteps and Lilian's agitated voice saying, "But, Mr. Sutton, you can't go—"

Antonia stared at Daniel. She felt as if her stomach had just plunged to her feet. It had been a week since she had seen him, and he looked at once different and yet dearly familiar. He looked unbelievably handsome to her, but there was a tired set to his features and a sadness in his eyes that made her want to cry. She had to clench all her muscles to keep from going to him.

"Daniel." Her voice came out a little rusty and hoarse. "I—you shouldn't be here."

"How else am I going to talk to you?" he asked reasonably. "You don't answer your phone, and you won't return any of my calls. You won't answer the door if I come by your house."

Antonia flushed and glanced at Mrs. Kritzer, who was listening to them avidly. She turned back to Daniel. "This isn't really the time.... I have patients...."

"Hello, Mrs. Kritzer," Daniel said, nodding toward her. "Sorry to interrupt."

"Hello, Daniel. How's your father?"

"Fine, ma'am. And you?"

"I'm doing very well, thank you."

They all continued to stand in a silent tableau, Daniel seemingly without any intent to move from the doorway, Mrs. Kritzer and Rita watching Antonia with great interest, and Antonia wishing she could magically disappear.

Finally she nodded toward the door, saying, "Let's

step out. If you'll excuse me, Mrs. Kritzer. Rita will get you those drops for Buster's ears.''

Both Rita's and Mrs. Kritzer's faces fell as they realized that they would miss the rest of the scene. Antonia started toward the door. Daniel stepped back, and she closed the door behind her.

In the hallway, Lilian was still standing near Daniel, and farther down, a whole waiting room full of people were peering down the hallway at them. Antonia muttered a curse.

''Why don't we take a walk?'' she said, and started down the hallway toward the back door, unbuttoning her white smock as she went and hanging it on a hook on the wall beside the door.

They stepped out into the parking lot, and Antonia turned toward the right, away from the veterinary building. There was a small park a couple of blocks away, and they started toward it, an awkward silence stretching between them.

Finally Daniel broke it, saying, ''I'm sorry. I shouldn't have interrupted you at work, but I didn't know what else to do. I had to talk to you, and you wouldn't give me a chance. I don't deserve that, Antonia.''

''I know,'' she said quickly, guilt gripping her. ''I know. I haven't been fair to you. I just couldn't talk to you. I—I've been too emotional.''

''It's okay to talk when you're emotional,'' he pointed out. ''Look, I want to apologize. I didn't mean to upset you. If I had known how you felt, I wouldn't have—it would have been hard, but I wouldn't have gone after him. I didn't realize that it would upset you.

You know, don't you, that I would never hurt *you.* I would never hit you. There's not a chance in hell you could ever make me angrier than Lurleen did, and I never even thought about hitting her. I am not a violent man."

"I'm not scared of you, Daniel. I know you wouldn't hurt me. It's not that. It was the way you took over, the way you decided what to do about it without even consulting me."

"I wanted to protect you."

"But don't you see? I have to take care of myself. It's my responsibility, not yours. I can't let you decide what's best for me."

"I don't want to try to run your life. I'm not like your ex-husband. I don't want to control you."

"I know you aren't like Alan." Antonia stopped and turned to face him. "You are a good, sweet man. But I cannot let others fight my battles for me anymore. I can't let someone else decide what's best for me or what I should do. I will not allow myself to sink back into that helpless, dependent person I used to be." Antonia repeated the arguments she had been telling herself the past few days whenever the pain of not being with Daniel grew too great and she was tempted to give in and call him.

"You won't be that way. Ever," Daniel said earnestly, taking her hand. He looked into her face, his dark eyes intense. "I would never try to make you that way. I love you just as you are. I realize that you are independent."

"But you took over anyway."

"I wasn't trying to take over. I wanted to help you.

I know that you could have handled it on your own. But what kind of person would I have been if I hadn't tried to help you? What kind of man? What kind of friend, let alone lover? Is that what you're looking for in a man? Someone who, if you're in trouble, would just step back and say, 'Hey, babe, that's your problem. You handle it.'''

Antonia stared at him, startled by the thought. "No, of course not. But—"

"But nothing," he said flatly. "What if the situation had been reversed, and I had been the one who was in trouble?"

"Don't be ridiculous."

"I'm not. Not an abusive spouse, obviously. But what if a horse had me pinned in a stall? What if a horse had thrown me? Would you just shrug and walk away, figuring I could take care of myself? After all, I'm an adult and capable of making my own decisions."

"Of course I would help you. But it's not the same!" Antonia cried.

"Why? What's the difference?"

"*You're* not helpless! *You* aren't weak! You don't have to prove yourself."

She stopped, aghast, her words lingering in the air.

"Neither do you," Daniel told her quietly. "You don't have to prove yourself to me or to anyone. I love you. When someone threatens you, I want to stop them. It's not wrong to help someone you love. Or to want to take care of them. That's not the same thing as stifling them or controlling them. I would never do those things to you. I don't want to do those things. I love you exactly as you are.''

Antonia moved away from him. She felt as if someone had just knocked the air out of her. ''I—I hadn't realized it until just now. But that's the real problem, isn't it? I'm helpless and weak.'' She turned to Daniel, her face white, tears pooling in her eyes. ''When Alan came after me, I didn't take care of it myself. I ran to you. Because I'm weak. That's why I'm scared to marry you. I keep thinking I can't get too close to you, I'll lose myself in you. I'll turn over all my problems to you. I'll give up my identity, my personhood.''

''No. That's crazy, Antonia.'' Daniel moved closer. ''You won't lose your identity at all. You'll still be you. Dr. Antonia Campbell. Hell, you don't have to take my name. Lots of other women do that, keep their own name. You don't even have to marry me if you don't want to. I just want to be with you. I want to go to sleep with you and wake up with you there beside me. But if that isn't what you want, I can live with it. We can just date. However you want it.''

Antonia closed her eyes, pain slicing through her at his description of the life he wanted with her. It was what she wanted, too, she realized, more than anything.

''I'm scared,'' she whispered. ''I'm scared I can't do it. I want to marry you. I want to be with you always. But what if I'm just too weak a person? It's not that you will take my identity away from me. Or that marriage will take it away. I'm scared that I'll just lose it, become a nothing. That I will give up my self because I don't have the strength or the courage to hold on to my identity. That's why I married Alan—because I was weak. I think I was looking for someone to control me because I wasn't able to myself. I attracted him because I'm helpless."

"Lady, you're talking crazy now," Daniel said firmly, taking hold of her arms and staring down into her eyes. "You listen to me. I don't know why you married Alan, because as far as I can see, he's an ugly little creep. And I don't know what attracted him to you. But I know what attracted me to you, and it sure as hell wasn't weakness. Why, the very first time I met you you practically took my head off for being a male chauvinist. Believe me, I didn't think, oh, what a nice, weak, malleable woman. You were tough, and I liked it. You still are.

"Look. You were married to an abusive man who did everything he could to take away your self-esteem, your pride, your will. But he couldn't do it. Sure, he managed to keep you down for a few years, but you didn't stay that way. You fought back. Even though you were scared, even though this man had terrorized you, you took action. You left him. You filed for divorce. You put your life back together. You went to school and became a vet, even though it's tough. I'm sure a lot of people tried to stop you from being a vet, but you didn't let them. And a lot of ignorant people, me included, tried to tell you you couldn't treat horses because you were a woman. But you didn't let that stop you either. And look at the way you fought him when Alan showed up at your house. You didn't cave in. You hit that son of a bitch and ran away from him.

Think about it. You aren't weak. You are one of the strongest people I know.''

Antonia stood looking at him, stunned. Daniel's words and her own sudden realization of how she had regarded herself these past few years had somehow opened up a door for her. She had been running scared, scared of her own weakness, her own incompetence. She felt as if a light had been switched on inside her. She remembered the sense of freedom she had felt the other day when Alan called her. Now she was feeling the same way, but far more powerfully. She didn't have to live in a box. She didn't have to guard herself against her own weakness. She was not weak at all, and as long as she kept on thinking that way, she was letting Alan control her life still. She was free and powerful in a way she had never let herself see before.

''Oh, Daniel!''

Antonia threw herself against him, her arms going tightly around his waist. She was trembling, and she wanted to burst into tears. At the same time, she wanted to laugh out loud.

''I love you,'' she whispered. ''I'm sorry. I've been an idiot.'' She leaned her head back and looked up at him. ''Not that I want you to decide things like that for me.''

''I understand,'' he responded promptly, his slow smile spreading across his lips. ''I promise. No decisions without consulting you. Scout's honor.''

''Good.''

Daniel kissed her, their lips clinging. Then he held her away from him a little, looking into her eyes.

"Does this mean we're okay again? You're taking me back?" he asked.

"More than that," Antonia said firmly. "It means I'm going to marry you."

Daniel chuckled. "Now that's what I like, Dr. Campbell—a woman who takes charge."

He pulled her back for another kiss, and Antonia melted into his arms.

* * * * *

HARLEQUIN "SILHOUETTE MAKES YOU A STAR!" CONTEST 1308
OFFICIAL RULES
NO PURCHASE NECESSARY TO ENTER

1. To enter, follow directions published in the offer to which you are responding. Contest begins June 1, 2001, and ends on September 28, 2001. Entries must be postmarked by September 28, 2001, and received by October 5, 2001. Enter by hand-printing (or typing) on an 8 ½" x 11" piece of paper your name, address (including zip code), contest number/name and attaching a script containing 500 words or less, along with drawings, photographs or magazine cutouts, or combinations thereof (i.e., collage) on no larger than 9" x 12" piece of paper, describing how the Silhouette books make romance come alive for you. Mail via first-class mail to: Harlequin "Silhouette Makes You a Star!" Contest 1308, (in the U.S.) P.O. Box 9069, Buffalo, NY 14269-9069, (in Canada) P.O. Box 637, Fort Erie, Ontario, Canada L2A 5X3. Limit one entry per person, household or organization.

2. Contests will be judged by a panel of members of the Harlequin editorial, marketing and public relations staff. Fifty percent of criteria will be judged against script and fifty percent will be judged against drawing, photographs and/or magazine cutouts. Judging criteria will be based on the following:

   - Sincerity—25%
   - Originality and Creativity—50%
   - Emotionally Compelling—25%

   In the event of a tie, duplicate prizes will be awarded. Decisions of the judges are final.

3. All entries become the property of Torstar Corp. and may be used for future promotional purposes. Entries will not be returned. No responsibility is assumed for lost, late, illegible, incomplete, inaccurate, nondelivered or misdirected mail.

4. Contest open only to residents of the U.S. (except Puerto Rico) and Canada who are 18 years of age or older, and is void wherever prohibited by law; all applicable laws and regulations apply. Any litigation within the Province of Quebec respecting the conduct or organization of a publicity contest may be submitted to the Régie des alcools, des courses et des jeux for a ruling. Any litigation respecting the awarding of a prize may be submitted to the Régie des alcools, des courses et des jeux only for the purpose of helping the parties reach a settlement. Employees and immediate family members of Torstar Corp. and D. L. Blair, Inc., their affiliates, subsidiaries and all other agencies, entities and persons connected with the use, marketing or conduct of this contest are not eligible to enter. Taxes on prizes are the sole responsibility of the winner. Acceptance of any prize offered constitutes permission to use winner's name, photograph or other likeness for the purposes of advertising, trade and promotion on behalf of Torstar Corp., its affiliates and subsidiaries without further compensation to the winner, unless prohibited by law.

5. Winner will be determined no later than November 30, 2001, and will be notified by mail. Winner will be required to sign and return an Affidavit of Eligibility/Release of Liability/Publicity Release form within 15 days after winner notification. Noncompliance within that time period may result in disqualification and an alternative winner may be selected. All travelers must execute a Release of Liability prior to ticketing and must possess required travel documents (e.g., passport, photo ID) where applicable. Trip must be booked by December 31, 2001, and completed within one year of notification. No substitution of prize permitted by winner. Torstar Corp. and D. L. Blair, Inc., their parents, affiliates and subsidiaries are not responsible for errors in printing of contest, entries and/or game pieces. In the event of printing or other errors that may result in unintended prize values or duplication of prizes, all affected game pieces or entries shall be null and void. **Purchase or acceptance of a product offer does not improve your chances of winning.**

6. Prizes: (1) Grand Prize—A 2-night/3-day trip for two (2) to New York City, including round-trip coach air transportation nearest winner's home and hotel accommodations (double occupancy) at The Plaza Hotel, a glamorous afternoon makeover at a trendy New York spa, $1,000 in U.S. spending money and an opportunity to have a professional photo taken and appear in a Silhouette advertisement (approximate retail value: $7,000). (10) Ten Runner-Up Prizes of gift packages (retail value $50 ea.). Prizes consist of only those items listed as part of the prize. Limit one prize per person. Prize is valued in U.S. currency.

7. For the name of the winner (available after December 31, 2001) send a self-addressed, stamped envelope to: Harlequin "Silhouette Makes You a Star!" Contest 1197 Winners, P.O. Box 4200 Blair, NE 68009-4200 or you may access the www.eHarlequin.com Web site through February 28, 2002.

Contest sponsored by Torstar Corp., P.O Box 9042, Buffalo, NY 14269-9042.

SRMYAS2

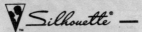

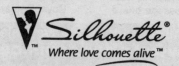